CW00541471

Dear Editor...

Dear Editor…
The collected letters of Oscar Brittle

Glenn Fowler, Christopher Smyth and Gareth Malone

With illustrations by
Andrew Joyner

NEW
SOUTH

A New South book

Published by
University of New South Wales Press Ltd
University of New South Wales
Sydney NSW 2052
AUSTRALIA
www.unswpress.com.au

© Glenn Fowler, Christopher Smyth & Gareth Malone 2009
First published 2009

This book is copyright. Apart from any fair dealing for the purpose
of private study, research, criticism or review, as permitted under
the Copyright Act, no part may be reproduced by any process
without written permission. Inquiries should be addressed to the
publisher.

National Library of Australia
Cataloguing-in-Publication entry
Author: Brittle, Oscar.
Title: Dear editor: the collected letters of Oscar Brittle/Glenn
    Fowler; Christopher Smyth; Gareth Malone.
ISBN: 978 1 74223 011 5 (hbk.)
Notes: Includes index.
Subjects: Brittle, Oscar – Correspondence.
        Newspaper editors – Correspondence.
        Newspaper publishing – Australia.
Other Authors/Contributors:
        Fowler, Glenn.
        Smyth, Christopher.
        Malone, Gareth.
Dewey Number: 808.86

Design Di Quick
Cover and all line drawings Andrew Joyner
Printer Ligare

This book is printed on paper using fibre supplied from plantation
or sustainably managed forests.

All reasonable efforts were taken to obtain permission to use
copyright material reproduced in this book, but in some cases
copyright holders could not be traced. The authors welcome
information in this regard.

As published by *The Australian*

MONDAY, FEBRUARY 27, 2006

THERE are so many things that make me cranky, I don't even know where to start.

Oscar Brittle
Killara, NSW

Preface

In early 2006, Oscar Brittle, a long-time resident of the leafy, established, neat, northern Sydney suburb of Killara, had something of an epiphany. Civilised society was going to hell in a hand-basket and he, for one, was not going to stand idly by. Driven by this awakened sense of civic pride, Brittle embarked on a bold campaign to wrest control of the debates in newspapers and magazines from the wishy-washies and weaklings. In the two years that followed, Oscar Brittle became (arguably) the most significant and powerful contributor to public debate in contemporary Australia.

Oscar Brittle might also be a delicate blend of Glenn Fowler, Christopher Smyth and Gareth Malone, who might still be pinching themselves that the ruse came off.

This book is a collection of published letters to editors, published replies from various correspondents, email exchanges between Oscar and editors, (inexplicably) rejected letters, the illustrations of Andrew Joyner and a few other little treats.

Once you've read Brittle, you will never read letters pages the same way again.

Some explanations

This project was designed to test the limits of what is publishable and what is not in the print media of Australia and beyond. The question posed is this: In an age when opinions are cropping up like weeds, what constitutes a *valid* opinion?

There was never any intention to offend, harm or humiliate, and it is sincerely hoped that the exercise is taken in the spirit in which it was intended. It is also hoped that this book inspires letter writers everywhere to persist in the face of rejection, secure in the knowledge that even the most incongruous letters will eventually get a guernsey.

The newspapers and magazines mentioned have no connection with the book's publication.

Where newspaper and magazine editors have made significant omissions from or amendments to the original submissions, these sections have been **bolded** in the accompanying text. Where letters appear in published form only, they have been published by newspapers and magazines without alteration.

In some cases, names have been removed, concealed or changed to protect the gullible.

Dear Editor,

A warning.

I have just drunk a full bottle of olive oil and I just had to tell someone about it. Please don't fall into the same trap as I did of assuming that the human body will pass gallstones if you consume a bottle of olive oil. I'm here to tell you it won't.

Yours sincerely
Oscar Brittle
Killara

ment – from council rates to state levies and federal taxes.

The review is a U-turn for Mr Costello, who last year scoffed at suggestions from the Sydney MP Malcolm Turnbull to "broaden the base and cut the rates".

Mr Costello told ABC television yesterday: "I'm trying to identify those areas where Australia lags so we can concentrate on them. Now nobody would say we've got a perfect tax system in Australia, so let's look around the world and let's see who does it better."

Hinting at the review's empha-

against calls to cut super taxes. Super concessions are already generous by world standards.

It will also give Mr Costello new ammunition to attack the NSW Government for failing to axe various "nuisance" taxes in return for GST revenue. It could conceivably give the Federal Government justification to raise the GST rate of 10 per cent to the higher levels in other countries. "You don't announce something like this and not follow through," said one source close to the project.

Mr Warburton, who is chair-

an "o

"Yo
woul
he in
refor

No
mit o
wide
tax s
sition
"You
with
on w

Anal
Edit

COLUMN **8** More – Page 16

'Don't fall into the same trap as I did of assuming that the human body will pass gallstones if you consume a bottle of olive oil,' says Oscar Brittle, of Killara. 'I'm here to tell you it won't.'

Too late for

A mother and her baby are de
history of domestic violence. W
prevented, ask **Paola Totaro** a

WEATHER Details – Page 14

- Sydney city showers 20°-24°
  Tomorrow fine 19°-25°

- Sydney west showers 18°-25°
  Tomorrow fine 18°-26°

MOLLY is just eight years old. Some time before 2am on a humid January night, she ran more than half a kilometre from her home in Hosking Crescent, Glenfield, past open parklands and into a darkened street nearby.

servic
Lynch
Maso
– suc
lation
Hospi
and
house

The Sydney Morning Herald

February 27, 2006   First published 1831 No. 52,557 $1.20

MISTRESS AND COMMANDER
Geena Davis's president arrives

Central Coast battlers set for grand final

'I wouldn't change my job'
Shot policewoman

Trade-off for tax cuts: lose your lurks

...RS are likely to lose ...nd deductions in for big personal cuts in ...er, following the first ...view of the tax system in ...20 years.

...deral Treasurer, Peter ... yesterday cleared the ... tax taxes and close loop- ... the system to bring it in ... international standards. ...s asked the business ...ck Warburton and Peter ...prepare an "authorit- ...ent" on how Australia's ... of federal taxes.

It will also give Mr Costello new ammunition to attack the NSW Government for failing to axe various "nuisance" taxes in return for GST revenue. It could conceivably give the federal Government justification to raise the GST rate of 10 per cent to the higher levels in other countries. "You don't announce something like this and not follow through," said one source close to the project.

Mr Warburton, who is chair-

man of the taxation board, and Mr Hendy who heads the Australian Chamber of Commerce and Industry, will specifically look at the spiralling costs of tax offsets, rebates, deductions and other "tax expenditures". They will also highlight where state and local governments may be overcharging, including payroll taxes, financial transaction duties and even development charges for new land releases.

Mr Hendy, an advocate of radical tax cuts for high earners, said: "Hopefully it will inform the Government when it makes some decisions for the May budget."

Insiders say the review provides Mr Costello with an "elegant dismount" from his previous resistance to tax reform. And, they said, it might have been timed to highlight his credentials in a week focused on John Howard's 10th anniversary as prime minister.

The Queensland backbencher Peter Slipper said the review was an "outstanding announcement".

"You'll find the Treasurer wouldn't have done this unless he intended to make meaningful reform," he said.

Not since Bob Hawke's Tax summit of 1985 has there been such a wide-ranging examination of the system. However, the Opposition Leader, Kim Beazley, said: "You don't need an inquiry to deal with that, you simply need to get on with it."

Mr Warburton, who is ...

Analysis – Page 2
Editorial – Page 8

Bubble and trouble: Tropfest cops a lashing

Dropped fest ... torrential rain brings misery in the Domain for festival fans last night; below, Rose Byrne before the soaking.   Photos: Lisa Wiltse

Alexa Moses

A SEVERE storm cut the 14th Tropfest film festival short last night and sent an estimated 35,000 people running for shelter.

With three of the 16 films still to be screened, organisers called off the event, citing safety concerns due to lightning.

The judges – including Toni Collette, Rose Byrne, Guy Pearce, Simon Baker and Phillip Noyce – were drenched in the teeming rain and took shelter in the VIP tents in the Domain.

Earlier in the night, as rain clouds threatened, organisers said the short film festival would go ahead "rain, hail or shine".

However, the audience started

leaving midway through the program at about 9.30 as torrential rain soaked the city.

The festival continued in Melbourne, Canberra, Brisbane, Perth and Hobart, and organisers expect to announce the winner today.

Elsewhere in Sydney, flooding caused cars to float and overwhelmed the drains in Penrith, closing roads there. Flooding also closed roads in St Marys and damaged homes in Northmead and Penrith.

Tropfest's program director, Serena Paull, said: "We've had rain before but never torrential rain like this. There's been a lightning storm and so we can't continue." She said the judges

would be provided with DVD copies of all 16 finalists to make their decision.

Before the downpour prematurely ended the night,

that haven't done their research. The festival has always been about trying ... people who haven't made ... the best possible film."

The theme of this year's Tropfest was bubbles, with every film needing to con... one to qualify.

The first prize includes a ... digital camera and a trip to ... Angeles to meet Hollywood ... executives. The winner will ... go to New York, where their ... will screen at the Tribeca F... Festival as part of the first international Tropfest.

Tropfest's director, John Polson, rejected claims it had lost its grassroots beginnings.

"I think it's crap," Polson said. "I think people who say

Get your free Tropfest DV... – Details, Page 4

Too late for Molly, but answers needed

A mother and her baby are dead after a long history of domestic violence. Why wasn't this prevented, ask Paola Totaro and Gwyn Topham.

MOLLY is just eight years old. Some time before 2am on a humid January night, she ran more than half a kilometre from her home in Hosking Crescent, Glenfield, past open parkland and into a darkened street nearby.

When a family friend, Wayne Smith, opened the door she screamed that her mum had told her to run, to run for her life.

Inside the fibro townhouse Molly shared with her mother, Adele Lynch, baby brother Mason and Aaron Reed – her mother's new boyfriend – a noisy and violent fight had been escalating for more than three hours.

Less than 45 minutes after Molly's flight, a triple-0 call was registered for the address. The townhouse was engulfed in flames. By the time emergency

services arrived about 3am, Ms Lynch lay dead inside while Mason – pulled out by a fire crew – succumbed to smoke inhalation not long after in Liverpool Hospital. Mr Reed, found gasping and screaming outside the house, died two days later.

Now, one month after the tragedy the fire – and what led to it – has become the subject of a coroner's inquiry and an internal police investigation amid claims that several frantic telephone calls from neighbours and friends to Macquarie Fields police were not taken seriously and that the police response was delayed.

But according to the series of events pieced together by the Herald this week, the tragedy reveals a much more complex story – one which is played out again and again in the Campbelltown

local government area, a district with the highest incidence of metropolitan domestic violence in the nation.

It is also a story where dysfunctional families, vulnerable children and burgeoning drug and alcohol abuse meet overworked police officers who can be worn down – and culturally hardened – by a social

problem that is growing dramatically but which is stripped for resources to help victims.

According to information collated by the Herald, about 11.20pm on January 21 police visited Ms Lynch's house after receiving a call from a person who said they lived nearby. It is understood that Ms Lynch met

Continued Page 4

Tragedy ... Adele Lynch with her children, Mason and Molly

Not a terrorist, but Jihad Jack guilty of taking al-Qaeda's cas...

Ian Munro

HE IS the white boy Osama bin Laden offered $10,000 to carry out an attack on Australia, and yesterday he became the first Australian to be convicted under the new counter-terrorism laws.

The Victorian Supreme Court found Joseph Thomas guilty of receiving funds from al-Qaeda and possessing a false passport, but he was acquitted on two charges of intentionally providing al-Qaeda resources.

Prosecutors had alleged he was a sleeper agent for bin Laden, but in an interview before his trial Thomas denied he ever intended to act against Australia.

"I might be naive and I might be an idealist but I am not a dickhead who will help to hurt innocent people," he said. "I am a fifth-generation Australian – 105 years, Irish-Australian. The offer to come home and be a sleeper

'OSAMA WANTS A WHITE BOY'

'He called me into the room and said: "If you know anyone who is willing to carry out an operation I can give them $10,000."'

Joseph Thomas reveals his al-Qaeda encounter. Page 10

agent where my family live is totally ridiculous."

The 32-year-old was hiding in a Pakistani safe house in 2002 when he was approached by one of al-Qaeda's inner circle, Khaled bin Attash, with the idea he run surveillance on Australian military bases. Just minutes before, bin Attash announced to several

people in the safe house that ... ralia should be attacked.

"I was not prepared to g ... assistance of the sort Kha ... Attash was on about," T ... said. "I believe Khaled bin ... saw my situation and used ... get up and said, 'Your mon ... ticket have been organised ... not accept the offer until ... subsequently."

The jury found Thomas ... of accepting $US3500 (t ... and a Qantas plane ticket ... He was also found guilty o ... ing his Pakistani visa to m ... look like he had been in ... gion for two weeks, inst ... $2\frac{1}{2}$ years. Thomas claim ... planned to use the mon ... Attash gave him to help ... ily and not for terrorism.

Significantly, jurors aske ... tice Philip Cummins durin ... deliberations why they ... been shown a notebook in ...

Continued Page 10

MN 8 News – Page 16

...fall into the same trap ...of assuming that the ...body will pass ...nes if you consume a ...of olive oil," says Oscar ...of Killara. "I'm here ...you it won't."

...HER Details – Page 14

...ly city showers 20°-24°
...rrow fine 19°-25°
...ly west showers 18°-23°
...rrow fine 18°-26°
...ly south showers 18°-23°
...rrow showers 19°-25°
...ngong showers 18°-23°
...rrow fine, cloudy 17°-23°

ISSN 0312-6315

70312 631018

Your money. Your terms.

ANZ Term Deposits • Flexible • Secure • Convenient • Simple • Reliable income

...% p.a on 7 month Term Deposits. For amounts $25,000 and over. Call us on 1800 008 177 or drop into any ANZ branch. More convenient banking. That's ANZ now.

Dear Editor,

I have it on good authority that some people's lives would fall apart without **'the Internet'**. Call me a Luddite, but **I'm here to say that I very much** prefer life without this **accursed** invention. **Such powerful words are the result of** several failed attempts on my behalf to become acquainted with **the 'W.W.W.'. Let me explain.**

Firstly, I was told that the Internet would **assist** me with some research that I am doing for my latest volume of poetry, entitled *Songs Without the Music*. I searched 'Martin Luther King', the great civil rights advocate, only to find that I was soon on a page **extrapolating** white supremacist **and anti-Semitic views. This caused me to almost choke on my mid-morning muffin!**

Next, I was encouraged by my nephew to obtain an 'e(lectric) mail address'. One week later, I had received no word from anyone I knew, but I had plenty of unsolicited messages **from sources such as 'Lloyds Bank', 'Quickie', 'Spank the Monkey', 'Kelvin', 'Doodles' and 'Fat Pud'.** One message even offered me a grossly overpriced 'penis extension'. Is there no shame left in the world?

And just this morning I discovered that some of the **W.W.W.** sites I wanted to look at required me to surrender my credit card details. The whole thing seems like a con to me.

Anyway, I was wondering if anyone out there has any information about shutting the Internet down for good – or is it too late? **My sister's friend Spiro is an electrician, and he has indicated to me that it shouldn't be too hard.** If the Internet causes more harm than good by poisoning people's minds, attacking their sense of common decency and emptying their purses, then what is the use of it?

Yours sincerely
Oscar Brittle
Killara

TUESDAY, MAY 9, 2006

Net leaves me cold

I have it on good authority that some people's lives would fall apart without the internet. Call me a Luddite, but I prefer life without this invention, after several failed attempts to become acquainted with it.

First, I was told that the internet would help me with some research that I am doing for my latest volume of poetry, titled *Songs Without the Music*. I searched for Martin Luther King, the great civil rights advocate, only to find that I was soon on a white supremacist page.

Next, I was encouraged by my nephew to obtain an email address. One week later, I had received no word from anyone I knew, but plenty of unsolicited messages. One even offered me a grossly overpriced penis extension. Is there no shame left in the world?

Now I discover some sites I wanted to look at require me to surrender credit card details. It all seems like a con.

Does anyone have any information about shutting the internet down for good – or is it too late? If the internet causes more harm than good by poisoning people's minds, attacking their sense of common decency and emptying their purses, then what use is it?

Oscar Brittle
Killara

Dear Editor,

Human organs and the like have been very much in the news lately, but do you realise that there are many parts of the human body that have ceased to serve any useful purpose? Most people know that we can live quite happily without the appendix (as our modern food is so well cooked), male nipples (now that women breast or bottle feed) and the tonsils (though the internet can't seem to explain that one). But only a select few know that, since we stopped climbing trees, toenails are now totally useless. I've actually had one removed and it saves me eleven seconds per week in cutting time! **(Fingernails, however, still aid personal grooming, especially nasal.)** Hair, once so useful in keeping the body and head warm **(see *Teen Wolf*),** has now been superseded by clothes and the beanie. Lots of people function perfectly well with only one kidney, and some have a smashing time without a spleen. Even arms and legs are of limited utility, as that Milton chap proves every time he skis down a mountain **faster than normal people.**

Indeed, if Darwin has got it right, we will soon evolve into hairless, nippleless torsos with bald, toothless heads - skiing fast, sitting mute and motionless in robot cars, and trading our brains in for smarter computers and larger television sets. I'm glad I won't be around to see it.

Yours sincerely
Oscar Brittle
Killara

Herald Sun

THURSDAY, AUGUST 24, 2006

Bits and pieces we can do without

HUMAN organs and the like have been very much in the news lately, but do you realise that there are many parts of the human body that have ceased to serve any useful purpose?

Most people know that we can live quite happily without the appendix (as our modern food is so well cooked), male nipples (now that women breast or bottle feed) and the tonsils (though the internet can't seem to explain that one).

But only a select few know that, since we stopped climbing trees, toenails are now totally useless. I've actually had one removed and it saves me 11 seconds a week in cutting time.

Hair, once so useful in keeping the body and head warm, has now been superseded by clothes and the beanie.

Lots of people function perfectly well with only one kidney, and some have a smashing time without a spleen.

Even arms and legs are of limited utility, as that Milton chap proves every time he skis down a mountain.

Indeed, if Darwin has got it right,

Far from disabled: one-legged Michael Milton at the Turin winter paralympics in March.

we will soon evolve into hairless, nippleless torsos with bald, toothless heads – skiing fast, sitting mute and motionless in robot cars and trading our brains in for smarter computers and larger television sets.

I'm glad I won't be around to see it.

Oscar Brittle
Killara, NSW

**Also published by *The Burnie Advocate* under the title
'We're evolving into thin air'**

e(lectric)mails

The editor from *The Burnie Advocate* emailed Oscar about his letter on human organs, asking him to give her a call and confirm authorship. Oscar replied with:

From: Brittle, Oscar
To: The Editor — The Burnie Advocate
Subject: Re: Your letter

Thank you, madam.

For reasons I would rather not discuss, I am unable to speak on the telephone. It is just too painful for me. That's why I like to write letters.

I guess that means you won't publish my work.

Yours sincerely
Oscar Brittle

The editor then emailed to say that she couldn't find an O. Brittle in the White Pages but, because the subject was not contentious, she had gone ahead and published his letter. Oscar replied:

From: Brittle, Oscar
To: The Editor — The Burnie Advocate
Subject: Re: Your letter

That's super! I guess by 'contentious' you may mean my Tasmanian Tiger letter, which I sent a few months ago.

Yours sincerely
Oscar Brittle

End of correspondence

Dear Editor,

I've been busy baking. I've been preparing a big batch of HUMBLE PIES for every 'scientist' who claims that the Tasmanian Tiger is extinct. Keep reading: you won't regret it!

Last Tuesday, as I was looking for fossils on my ninety-acre holiday property just south of Burnie, I saw a tall rodent-like creature dive into the undergrowth at the sound of my impending approach. I know it was a Tasmanian Tiger, because I have seen one on an old newsreel, and when I shot at this one it seemed to move in a *very* similar fashion. Animals react consistently to fear, or so I have read. Also, it had stripes, like all members of the tiger family.

Anyway, I set my hounds on to the beast, and although they were not speedy enough to bring it down, they led me to some very interesting paw prints. Over the page is a quick sketch of what they looked like …

(Sketch by O. Brittle, using computer)

I am publicising my find in the hope that somebody of note contacts me. As far as I know, an animal needs to have no confirmed sightings in 70 years to be classified as extinct, and, by my calculations, I have just snuck in.

The fallacy that we have lost the Tasmanian Tiger, like the animal itself, cannot be allowed to thrive. It is a scandal, and this is not a term I like to bandy about loosely.

Yours sincerely
Oscar Brittle
Killara

e(lectric)mails

From: Brittle, Oscar
To: The Editor – The Burnie Advocate
Subject: Phone Call

Hello there!

My wife tells me there was a telephone message from somebody at the Burnie Advocate. I am 'O.S.' at the moment so I couldn't return your call. Will you be publishing my letter?

Yours sincerely
Oscar Brittle
Killara

The editor from *The Burnie Advocate* responded to say that the letter would now be considered for publication.

Dear Editor,

The world has bought itself a one-way ticket to oblivion. Here's proof …

On the Thursday evening before last, I did what I rarely do: I ventured outside the four walls of my studio to see what was transpiring on streets roamed by the weak. The mood was as I remembered it – chaotic, confused and pre-apocalyptic. I steeled myself and pushed on.

In the hours that followed I saw many alarming things. I saw rats fighting cats, cats fighting dogs, dogs fighting men and men fighting rats, and I saw people watching these fights with cynical smiles on their faces and indifferent grunts escaping from their cracked lips. I saw a plain old crone screaming foul words at a hirsute greengrocer, who had allegedly overcharged her for a cantaloupe. I saw sprinklers turned on in the rain. I saw a man running for a bus which did not stop. I saw a woman without legs changing the tyre on her wheelchair, while others passed on the busy thoroughfare, eager to get to their next wrestling match or Art Nouveau film. I saw a sunset blocked by post-modern monstrosities that had long since dwarfed the cathedrals. I smelt vomit and excreta where once I would have smelt frangipanis and lavender. I felt a chilling wind on a night when meteorologists had predicted nothing of the sort. I slipped on loose gravel and bruised my coccyx.

Before I limped to the sanctity of my home, where I would embrace my Schnauzer Charlie and promise him (with no real confidence) that I would protect him from the swelling hordes of miscreants, I stepped into the shadows and did the only thing that a sane person could have done in the circumstances.

I wept.

Yours sincerely
Oscar Brittle
Killara

by *The Northern Territory News*

The Sydney Morning Herald

Devolutionary theory

I entered the men's toilets of a suburban shopping mall recently to find faeces smeared on the walls and floor. Charles Darwin was a brilliant man and his ideas have revolutionised human thought. I suspect, however, that his thesis did not go far enough. My reading of Darwin's *Origin of Species* is that humans will continue to evolve and improve. I beg to differ.

I think we have reached our peak (probably with the moon landing of 1969) and that we are on the way back down the evolutionary scale.

Put simply, we are becoming more ape-like. One can see it in contemporary dance moves, in porno films, in the proliferation of men with hairy shoulders and, of course, in the piles of plop caked on the walls and floors of suburban shopping mall toilets.

Oscar Brittle
Killara

The Sydney Morning Herald

WEDNESDAY, APRIL 5, 2006

Backtracking

I agree wholeheartedly with Oscar Brittle (*Letters*, April 3) that the human race has passed its evolutionary peak, but I believe he is being too generous by half to contemporary society in nominating the moon landing year of 1969 as the probable apex of our development.

I would have thought we reached the top of our evolutionary trajectory between 200 and 400 years ago – that is, somewhere around the lifetimes of Mozart, Shakespeare and Rembrandt.

Peter Austin
Mt Victoria

Oscar Brittle claims, among other things, that 'the proliferation of men with hairy shoulders' is a sign of humanity regressing in evolutionary terms.

Does that mean if I get rid of the hair on my back and shoulders, my cerebral cortex will become even larger, suddenly moving me a notch up the evolutionary scale?

Abdul Hamid Saad
Condell Park

The Sydney Morning Herald

THURSDAY, APRIL 6, 2006

Warney, top of the tree

I would be more precise than Peter Austin (*Letters*, April 5), and locate the apex of human (or at least, Western) political achievement in the late 18th century. This was the time of Jean-Jacques Rousseau, Edward Gibbon, Thomas Jefferson and Benjamin Franklin, when the idea of individual liberation was born and flourished in the American and French revolutions.

Things went a bit haywire in France not long after, resulting in the Terror, and the Empire. In the US, however, it wasn't until the 2004 election that we saw the death of the Enlightenment.

Ken Fraser
Armidale

I think Oscar Brittle and Peter Austin are both wrong (*Letters*, April 3, 5). According to Jacob Bronowski in *The Ascent of Man*, man's progress to his evolutionary peak is conditioned by 'the refinement of the hand in action'.

Given the diversity of skills his fingers have developed both on and off the field, this would mean that Shane Warne would be much closer to the apex than a Shakespeare or a Mozart.

David Grant
Ballina

Dear Editor,

THE POWER TO DREAM.

The world is overcrowded. My response to this has always
been: 'Welcome to my universe'.

It's Brittlonia, where no-one is cold and no-one is born
and no-one complains or ever wants to leave. There are 3
gods and 9 suns. Illness is just a display in a dusty museum
and loneliness so rare that even the right to feel it is
auctioned amongst the super-rich, the proceeds of which are
lavished on the homeless. Random breath tests are conducted
with chocolate cigarettes and, in place of water, warm honey
drips slowly from every tap.

The point I am trying to make is quite simple: that
with the power to dream, changes can be made and unseen
possibilities will arrive into thrilling view!

Yours sincerely
Oscar Brittle
Killara

by *The Communist Party Guardian*

Parramatta Sun

WEDNESDAY, MARCH 1, 2006

The pain of pesto

Civic duty has prompted me to put pen to paper, something my cursed arthritic hands usually prevent me from doing. But these days pain is my only companion.

My troubles began at my local church fete. The parish operates a modest cake and condiments stall and it was here that I purchased a jar labelled simply pesto – $3.25. It may have cost me only $3.25, but the price I've paid for consuming that ghastly paste has been considerably higher.

After leaving said fete, I quietly instructed my wife to prepare for me a potful of tagliatelle through which I liberally stirred the green confection.

Only minutes after finishing my lunch I began to experience powerful feelings of euphoria, bouts of hilarity and insatiable hunger. And so I went, spoon in hand, back to the jar of pesto and gobbled the remains. My only recollection of the events that followed is a kaleidoscopic montage best described as Rabelaisian. I certainly don't remember picking up the broom or returning to the fete to buy more pesto and lamingtons.

Dignity prevents me from detailing here what the brethren have recounted to me about my actions during the four hours I roamed – suffice to say that for a man whose only tipple is the occasional sherry with his afternoon crumpet, I am devastated by the apparent loss of my faculties.

I ask the following:

1. That there be stricter controls on unorthodox church produce.

2. That the Food and Drug Administration immediately mandate warnings on pesto and pesto-related products.

3. That the photographs your staff photographer took that afternoon be shredded.

Oscar Brittle
Killara

Dear Editor,

Once again, it's time the Chancellor reviewed our legal tender denominations.
     Recently, due largely to the effects of economic rationalism, inflation and interest rate increases, the five-cent piece has become practically redundant. I'm told that five-cent coins are no longer accepted in parking meters, toll booths or fruit machines and that their only practical use is for keel ballast and tracking chukkas on the polo field. Some years ago I had so many five-cent pieces littering my house that I quietly instructed my house-keeper to discard the things on site. **(I would have smelted them were it legal.)** I, like so many of the cash-rich, simply detest coinage. I predict that the ten-cent piece will soon follow the five into numismatic oblivion **(like the conch shell before them)** and propose that both the five- and ten-cent pieces be removed from the current monetary system post-haste. In their place I suggest two new coins be substituted - a 75-cent piece and a 99-cent piece. Ideal for that $49.75 cigar or $69.99 shoe tree, **these very practical alternatives would be called the 'Kerr' and the 'Bradman' respectively.** I've made some discreet inquiries and understand **that retooling the Royal Australian Mint to produce these new coins would be a very simple procedure and that** the old ten-cent coins could be sold to New Zealand in order to pay for the refit.
     My final request is for the rapid introduction of the 200 and 500 dollar notes. Personally I did away with using five, ten and twenty dollar notes years ago. Sentimentality aside, it amuses me that they are still in existence.

Yours sincerely
Oscar Brittle
Killara

Coin is a blasted nuisance

Recently, due largely to the effects of economic rationalism, inflation and interest-rate increases, the five-cent piece has become practically redundant (*Letters*, April 9). I'm told it is no longer accepted in parking meters, toll booths or fruit machines and that the only practical use is for keel ballast and tracking chukkas on the polo field.

Some years ago I had so many five-cent pieces littering my house that I quietly instructed my housekeeper to discard the things on sight. I, like so many of the cash-rich, simply detest coinage. I predict the 10-cent piece will soon follow the five into numismatic oblivion and propose that the five- and 10-cent pieces be removed from the monetary system post-haste. I suggest two new coins – a 75-cent piece and a 99-cent piece. Ideal for that $49.75 cigar or $69.99 shoe tree. I've made some discreet inquiries and understand the old 10-cent coins could be sold to New Zealand to pay for the refit.

Oscar Brittle
Killara

Dear Editor,

There seems to be a lot of debate at the moment surrounding capital punishment, but, to my mind, this debate seems to be a little misguided. Surely the issue is not whether or not we should have capital punishment: all sensible people know that we should. In actual fact, the debate should be centred on the extent to which this facility should be broadened.

So, what crimes should lead to instant death? Murder, of course, and certainly rape, kidnapping, _____, arson, terrorism, _____, communism, _____, _____ and grand theft. (You fill in the blanks for your readers. I trust you.)

Look, Editor, I'm not claiming to have all the answers: I just want to ask the questions. The alternative, I'm afraid, is for the whole ruddy lot of us to go straight to hell in a handbasket.

Yours sincerely
Oscar Brittle
Killara

by *The Daily Telegraph*

The Irrigator

FRIDAY, MAY 12, 2006

Confounding the wise

I HAVE decided to devote the remainder of my life to baffling future archaeologists, and I wonder if any of your readers (I'm a pseudo local at Leeton these days) would be prepared to join me in this elaborate ruse.

Too often I have sat down to watch a news report, such as the one this week about a 'new' dinosaur, only to have my sense of probity insulted by some smarmy archaeologist or paleontologist or some such thing who thinks he or she knows it all.

As the proponents of the Intelligent Design theory have recently demonstrated, it is highly unlikely that he or she does (know it all). I abhor the arrogance of archaeologists and I wish to confound and embarrass them.

Here's the plan I've hatched:

When my time comes, I will be buried in my own back yard in an enormous underground chamber, which my wife is currently digging.

The crypt will contain my headless corpse, a Great War pistol, a 19th-century sewing machine, an Ottoman ottoman, the skull of a dodo, a map of Mongolia, a Roman vase (don't worry, I've got one) and a pile of coins ranging in antiquity from the 1880s to the year of my death. Let's see them work out that lot.

My long-term goal is to teach archaeologists the lesson that not everything can be explained logically.

I encourage all like-minded individuals to incorporate similar plans into their lives.

Oscar Brittle
Killara

Dear Editor,

There are two major problems in this world: criminals and mosquitoes. (Correct me if I'm wrong.)

What bamboozles me is why, in the sacred name of Jesus, we don't set the former the task of destroying the latter.

Instead of sitting on their bottoms in gaol, playing basketball or backgammon, or converting to Islam even, these louts should be on supervised mosquito patrols/hunts. Look at the benefits: exercise and fresh air for the recalcitrants and guards, and the gradual decline of mosquito populations.

The last of these reasons will become even more crucial in years to come. Those of us who read are aware that the gigantic hole in the 'o zone layer' will make things hotter, and nasty things like dengue fever and malaria will work their way south.

That's why I'm calling on you, Townsville, to introduce this pilot program first. Fever, we know, is just around the corner. And so is your local gaol.

So, get the crims into some sun smart outfits, chain them appropriately, and give them some heavy-duty pesticide. Tell them to start at the swamps. That's where they breed.

I'll finish by saying this: Mosquitoes serve no useful purpose, but surely there is some hope left for the criminals.

Yours sincerely
Oscar Brittle
Killara

by *The Townsville Bulletin*

As published by *The Daily Telegraph*

FRIDAY, JULY 14, 2006

Road warriors

Whatever happened to manners on the road? At present, there seem to be more road ragers than ever – especially in Sydney's northern suburbs.

In the immediate post-war years, drivers in this area were known for their tolerance and patience. In recent months, I have had the middle finger raised (or the bird flipped, as my grandson puts it) more than a dozen times, I have been called the 'f' word probably twice that, I have been treated to three bare backsides, and I have been followed home by two louts who proceeded to hurl a beer bottle and half-chewed hamburger at my parked Rover.

Maybe my wife is right – it's time to catch the bus.

Oscar Brittle
Killara

MONDAY, JULY 17, 2006

In response to Oscar Brittle ('Road warriors,' *Letters*, July 14), I am a regular driver on the North Shore and although you encounter the odd madman and woman on the roads, I have never been witness to even a fraction of the abuse Mr Brittle seems to have been subject to over the last few months.

Perhaps it may be time for Mr Brittle to look at the way he drives. He must be doing something to attract all this attention.

Brett Dunne
Umina

e(lectric)mails

From: Roland, Les
To: Brittle, Oscar
Subject: The Sydney Magazine

My name is Les Roland and I'm preparing a feature for *The Sydney Morning Herald*'s 'Sydney Magazine' on 'Is Sydney a Rude City?' The Letters Editor at the magazine passed on your letter concerning your experiences at the hands of Road Ragers. As it is such an excellent example of the rudeness and incivility that occurs in this city these days, I'm contacting you to ask if I can incorporate your letter in my story.

I look forward to your response.

Yours sincerely
Les

From: Brittle, Oscar
To: Roland, Les
Subject: Re: The Sydney Magazine

That will be fine, Mr Roland. Would it be possible to let me know the exact edition? I usually get The (Sydney) Mag, but I must be sure not to miss this one.

Yours sincerely
Oscar Brittle
Killara

From: Roland, Les
To: Brittle, Oscar
Subject: Re: The Sydney Magazine

Hi Oscar,

Many thanks for letting me use your excellent letter in my story. It really says what many people are thinking out there.

Best regards
Les

Dear Editor,

As an advocate of reducing greenhouse gas emissions, I have long extolled the virtues of public transport (and worm farms). Now it seems this has been without foundation.

In an attempt to reduce my ecological footprint, I decided to leave the Range Rover at home last Thursday – **opting instead for omnibus transportation** into town. The morning trip was pleasant enough, as I sat next to a handsome, lightly perfumed young woman, read the paper and even attempted a **sudoki** puzzle. The journey home that evening was anything but satisfactory. I found myself squeezed into a seat without ample leg room and was subjected to the crazed ramblings of a Mediterranean gentleman sitting behind me, talking too loudly into his mobile **(telephone)**. Two large, shaven-headed women, **one of which I suspect may have been lesbian, boarded and** sat **in close proximity** to me, nonchalantly consuming hot potato chips and thereby displaying little consideration for me or other passengers. They wore no shoes. On arriving home, I sought solace in a double-header Pimms **I had my wife prepare** – such was the state of my nerves.

If Premier **Maurice** Iemma is serious about solving the public transport problem in this city, **might I suggest** he starts by making bus and train travel a more attractive proposition **for people like myself. Tomorrow** I, **and I suspect many of my ilk**, will once again firmly stamp my ecological feet and take the car to town. I will continue to do so until something is done. Climate change is one thing, but passenger comfort is not to be undervalued.

Yours sincerely
Oscar Brittle
Killara

TUESDAY, OCTOBER 24, 2006

Once was enough

As an advocate of reducing greenhouse gas emissions, I have long extolled the virtues of public transport (and worm farms). Now it seems this has been without foundation.

In an attempt to reduce my ecological footprint, I decided to leave the Range Rover at home last Thursday and catch the bus into town.

The morning trip was pleasant enough, as I sat next to a handsome, lightly perfumed young woman, read the paper and even attempted a Sudoku puzzle.

But the journey home that evening was anything but satisfactory. I found myself squeezed into a seat without ample leg room and was subjected to the crazed ramblings of a Mediterranean gentleman sitting behind me, talking too loudly into his mobile phone.

Two large, shaven-headed women sat close to me, nonchalantly consuming hot potato chips and thereby displaying little consideration for me or other passengers. They wore no shoes.

On arriving home, I sought solace in a double-header Pimms, such was the state of my nerves.

If Premier Morris Iemma is serious about solving the public transport problem in this city, he might start by making bus and train travel a more attractive proposition.

From now on, I will once again firmly stamp my ecological feet and take the car to town. I will continue to do so until something is done.

Climate change is one thing, but passenger comfort is not to be undervalued.

Oscar Brittle
Killara

WEDNESDAY, OCTOBER 25, 2006

Anyone can ride

In response to Oscar Brittle ('Once was enough,' *Letters*, October 24), public transport is exactly that – it gets you from A to B for a cheap fare.

Anybody can use it: good-looking, perfumed young women, large shaven-headed women, even the odd Mediterranean man. As far as I know there is no law that compels people to wear footwear.

The only thing I and many other commuters would object to would be sharing the public transport system with an arrogant toff such as Oscar Brittle, who should try to be more flexible.

Arthur Brown
Blair Athol

North Shore Times

FRIDAY, OCTOBER 27, 2006

Little comfort on public transport

AS an advocate of reducing greenhouse gas emissions, I have long extolled the virtues of public transport (and worm farms).

Now it seems this has been without foundation.

In an attempt to reduce my ecological footprint, I decided to leave the Range Rover at home last Thursday – opting instead for omnibus transportation into town.

The morning trip was pleasant enough.

The journey home that evening was anything but satisfactory.

I found myself squeezed into a seat without ample leg room and was subjected to the crazed ramblings of a gentleman sitting behind me, talking too loudly into his mobile (telephone).

Two large women boarded and sat in close proximity to me, nonchalantly consuming hot potato chips and thereby displaying little consideration for me or other passengers.

On arriving home, I sought solace in a double-header Pimms I had my wife prepare, such was the state of my nerves.

If Premier Iemma is serious about solving the public transport problem in this city, might I suggest he starts by making bus and train travel a more attractive proposition for people like myself.

Tomorrow I, and I suspect many of my ilk, will once again firmly stamp my ecological feet and take the car to town.

I will continue to do so until something is done.

Climate change is one thing, but passenger comfort is not to be under-valued.

Oscar Brittle
Killara

North Shore Times

WEDNESDAY, NOVEMBER 1, 2006

A BIG thanks to whoever wrote in as 'Oscar Brittle' (*Times*, October 27). Their caricature brought a much needed lightness to an otherwise dry letters page. I'd like to see a return of this heroic character, possibly telling us how he supports the fight against obesity but can't actually be bothered doing any exercise.

Adam Farrow-Palmer
Lane Cove

FRIDAY, NOVEMBER 3, 2006

YOUR correspondent Oscar Brittle appears to be insincere in describing himself as an advocate of reducing greenhouse gas emissions if his return trip on public transport offended his sensibilities so badly that he returned to his Range Rover. He describes the morning trip on the bus as quite pleasant but the return trip with a variety of fellow citizens using the public transport system was too much for him. How pathetic. Perhaps the government could fund single cubicles to shield people like Mr Brittle from talkative (perhaps friendly) men or plump women who dare to eat chips on public transport. It is this sort of thoughtlessness and selfishness that is putting our children, grandchildren and our country in the dangerous position it is in with global warming. I am pleased he was able to recover from his traumatic trip by getting the little woman to pour him his drink. I would have poured it over his head.

Margaret Atkin
Lindfield

Australian
Traveller
HONESTLY AUSTRALIAN

AUGUST/SEPTEMBER 2007

One of the stranger ones

Dear Editor. I am outside. I haven't been inside (my home) for three days and almost one night. It's raining.

My mind is filled with doubts and questions that have no end or beginning or meaning and still it rains on. I don't even know the name of the cyber-cafe I am in, but I know I am a wanderer. Another lost citizen of this global planet. Just one of the tomorrow people.

PS: Please advise of publication date. My brother needs to know.

Oscar Brittle
Killara NSW

Wow. Anyone else out there feeling like this? Don't worry – it's the winter. Summer will be back soon. ***Just hang in there. – Greg Barton, Ed.***

Dear Editor,

I'm all for democracy – don't get me wrong – but have you
ever thought it strange that every single person's vote has
exactly the same value? I'll put it this way: Rhodes Scholars
and CEOs have no more say in the result of an election than
somebody who has never read *The New Yorker* or *The Lancet*
or *The Endeavour Journals*, or who listens to country music,
or who insists on wearing one of those 'mullet' hairstyles.
This strikes me as grossly unfair, so much so that I have
devised a system which I would thank you and your readers
to seriously consider.

The system:

Every citizen over the age of 18 may vote. They are
awarded between one and ten votes each, depending upon
intellect, output and standing within the community.
Men of genius like Barry Jones or Andrew Peacock would
undoubtedly have the maximum ten votes. James Packer, Dame
Joan Sutherland or I – good salt-of-the-earth types - would
have eight or nine. Bankers and heroes of the people like
Russell Crowe would have six or seven votes. Soap stars
and pop singers would have four or five votes; golfers
and cricketers three; netballers, teachers, footballers
and nurses two. Anyone who listens to 'hop hop', races
greyhounds or attends the Royal Easter Show's sideshow alley
would have the basic single vote.

Obviously, these categorisations are fairly rough
(determined by me over a well-poured whiskey) and would
need to be nailed down in a firmer fashion by some sort of
committee. I recommend the Chancellor (Costello) to head
such a group. He has always struck me as a sensible man.

Yours sincerely
Oscar Brittle
Killara

by *The Cooma-Monaro Express*

Dear Editor,

As an old 'ad man', I've been quite impressed in recent years at the creativity of those in the advertising game. Ads that appear on private motor vehicles **(by negotiation with the owner of course)**, on polystyrene coffee cups, above urinals and on football coaches' shirt collars are all recent recipients of my commendation. And hats off to those involved in the SPAM revolution!

However, I get the sense that the ad boys **(and even girls these days)** have not even shifted into third gear on this stuff. There are just so many places left in society where advertisements are yet to appear.

Product placement in films is well and good, but what about novels, paintings, sculptures and theatrical sets?

Have they considered placing advertisements on restaurant plates or napkins? On hospital sheets or ceilings? What about placing ads on rear-vision mirrors? On cigarettes? On headstones? On pets? On other ads? On money itself?!

Why am I surrendering all of these innovative ideas? Well, I'm happily retired these days, but that doesn't stop me loving the ad game. I just want the young folk to do it better **and better**.

Yours sincerely
Oscar Brittle
Killara

AdNews

FEBRUARY 23, 2007

Wasted ad spaces

As an old 'ad man', I've been impressed in recent years at the creativity of those in the ad game. Ads that appear on private motor vehicles, on polystyrene coffee cups, above urinals and on football coaches' shirt collars are all recipients of my commendation. And, hats off to those involved in the SPAM revolution!

However, I get the sense that the ad boys and girls have not even shifted into third gear on this stuff. There are just so many places left in society where advertisements are yet to appear. Product placement in films is well and good, but what about novels, painting, sculptures and theatrical sets?

Have they considered placing ads on restaurant plates or napkins? On hospital sheets or ceilings? What about placing ads on rear-vision mirrors? On cigarettes? On gravestones? On pets? On other ads? On money itself? Why am I surrendering all of these innovative ideas? Well, I'm happily retired these days, but that doesn't stop me loving the ad game. I just want the young folk to do it even better.

Oscar Brittle
Retired ad man

Dear Editor,

In the days before police radar and speed cameras, it was easy to improve one's travel times between metropolitan centres. Today, the politicians and police have made it far more difficult for anyone interested in breaking the speed limit to set records. Some call this progress. I call it a minor inconvenience and have dedicated the last ten years of my life to devising ways of improving travel times without breaking the law. Here are some tips:

1. Coat your car's chassis in canola oil or cooking grease. This reduces drag.

2. Travel in the middle of the day. If the road is hot, your tyres should 'stick' when negotiating tricky corners. Also, warm up the tyres for 30 minutes before driving.

3. Remove accessories such as hubcaps, fog lights, tow bars, air bags, handbrake, rear wiper, spare tyre and jack, all of which add to the weight of the vehicle.

4. Strip down to your underpants. Clothing also adds to the weight of the vehicle.

5. If you are a parent, have your dependents catch the train or bus. This way you can remove the back seat, thereby reducing the car's weight even further.

Your readers should know that on a recent trip from Sydney to Bowral I managed to shave one minute and forty seconds off my personal best time. And I have the aforementioned methods to thank for it.

Yours sincerely
Oscar Brittle
Killara

by *The Open Road*

Dear Editor,

So, pole dancing is becoming fashionable.
    Well, I have been quietly pole dancing since the age of 15. I was taught this arcane art by my great uncle, and mastered all elements including whittling of the pole, singing and even sewing my own bonnet.
    After enduring ridicule at every public display, I learnt to keep my skill a secret until, after many years, I rose to the ancient Celtic rank of Sun Lizard.
    So, who's laughing now?

Yours sincerely
Oscar Brittle
Killara

by *The Herald Sun*

Dear Editor,

I see that Chief Minister Jon Stanhope has been soliciting Sydneysiders this week, extolling the virtues of Canberra in the hope of luring them to your fine city.

I am not a man who is known for outward displays of emotion **(they appal me)** but I'm not too proud to tell you, **via correspondence,** that what I saw in the nation's capital on the weekend **penetrated even my normally resilient defences and** was reason enough for me to seriously consider a move south.

It was nine minutes before dusk as I drove west along Hindmarsh**'s** Drive. I crested the hill **(name unknown)** and the full splendour of the Brindabella Ranges came into view, ambushing me in a full-blown assault on my senses. I was unprepared. The crimson sunset, the azure mountains and the verdant green hills combined in a rich tapestry of colour that was, quite simply, overwhelming.

Dear Editor, I wept.

I wept like I used to in the 80's.

Thank you.

Yours sincerely
Oscar Brittle
Killara

The Canberra Times

FRIDAY, APRIL 7, 2006

A wonderful city

I see that Jon Stanhope has been soliciting Sydneysiders this week, extolling the virtues of Canberra in the hope of luring them to your fine city.

I'm not a man who is known for outward displays of emotion but I'm not too proud to tell you that what I experienced in the nation's capital on the weekend was reason enough for me to seriously consider a move south.

It was nine minutes before dusk as I drove west along Hindmarsh Drive.

I crested the hill and the full splendour of the Brindabella Ranges came into view – ambushing me in a full-blown assault on my senses.

I was unprepared. The crimson sunset, the azure mountains and the verdant green hills combined, forming a rich tapestry of colour that was, quite simply, overwhelming. I wept. I wept like I used to in the '80s. Thank you.

Oscar Brittle
Killara NSW

Dear Editor,

The other day, an odd woman walked past me in the shops and asked: 'What is that smell?'

Without hesitation, I replied: 'That, my dear, is the smell of success'.

One-nil to Brittle, I believe.

Yours sincerely
Oscar Brittle
Killara

by 'Column 8', *The Sydney Morning Herald*

Dear Editor,

I have recently been self-diagnosed with prostrate cancer
- thanks to the electric Internet and some gentle prodding.
However, I still have a few questions. How can I skip the
middleman and convince a surgeon to go ahead and operate?
Or is it possible to 'self-medicate' in these situations and
remove the wretched gland myself? I'm very tempted by the
latter, I must admit.

Yours sincerely
Oscar Brittle
Killara

by *New Idea* magazine

Dear Editor,

What is happening to the youth of today? Please don't answer this question until you have read this letter.

I have just taken up a post as a music teacher at a Western Sydney high school. The other day I got to thinking: Why is it that so many of the children these days insist on listening to 'rap' music from America and reading 'Manga' comics from Japan? Why can't they take an interest in something Australian?!

So, I started an Australian Folk Song Club. My idea was to have a group of students join with me on stages all around the Greater West, performing classic songs such as 'Waltzing Matilda', 'Botany Bay' and 'Click Go the Sheers'. We could, I thought, even perform ditties like 'Old Man Emu' **and 'There was a Red Back on the toilet seat when I was there last night'** just to keep the kids happy. We could even wear colonial costumes and work in some amateur theatrics.

Anyway, the reason I am writing this letter is that when I advertised the first meeting of this new club to the students, I got absolutely no takers. NOT A BEAN! At this moment, I'm thinking of giving up.

Help!

Yours sincerely
Oscar Brittle
Killara

As published by *The Daily Telegraph*

MONDAY, MARCH 27, 2006

Folk songs fall flat

What is happening to the youth of today? Please don't answer that question until you have read this letter.

I have just taken up a post as a music teacher at a Western Sydney high school. The other day I got to thinking: why is it that so many of the children these days insist on listening to rap music from the US and reading Manga comics from Japan? Why can't they take an interest in something Australian?

So, I started an Australian folk song club. My idea was to have a group of students join me on stages all around the Greater West, performing classic songs such as *Waltzing Matilda, Botany Bay* and *Click Go The Shears*. We could, I thought, even perform ditties such as *Old Man Emu*, just to keep the kids happy. We could even wear colonial costumes and work in some amateur theatrics.

But when I advertised the first meeting of this new club to the students, I got absolutely no takers. Not a bean. At this moment, I'm thinking of giving up.

Oscar Brittle
Killara

WEDNESDAY, MARCH 29, 2006

Old folk

In response to Oscar Brittle ('Folk songs fall flat,' *Letters*, March 27), why should young people today be interested in folk songs from a bygone era?

Click Go The Shears indeed. By all means try to get rid of rap music from the US and Manga comics from Japan, but offer something Australian that is current and you might get some takers.

I'm in my sixties, but am well aware that a lot of people of this vintage live in the past. Young people are forward-thinking, and so they should be.

Mr Brittle is living in the past. Consider the era in which these young people were born and you will perhaps understand their perspective on life.

Irene Bergstrom
Lane Cove

Dear Editor,

In his merciless attack on Australian folk songs, Irene Bergstrom ('Old folk', *Letters*, March 29) implies that if something is not modern it is without value and can be discarded. If we followed that logic, we could give the chop to all manner of things Australians first held dear in the 1800s: test cricket, the bicycle and the study of Latin. Mr Bergstrom accuses me of 'living in the past'. Well, if this involves owning an iPod, listening to Keith Urban and dancing street funk, then I am guilty as charged, but it doesn't stop me from singing *The Wild Colonial Boy*! There is something to be said for not giving young people what they *want*, but what they *need*.

Yours sincerely
Oscar Brittle
Killara

by *The Daily Telegraph*

Dear Editor,

After six years of painstaking research, I am able to conclude that all of the world's conspiracy theories are the work of one man. That man is Derek Ronald Jenkins of 12 Millwood Lane, Cambridge, United Kingdom. (Block out the address if you need to.)

Facts simply do not lie.

Jenkins has been placed at the scene of some of the most newsworthy events of the last fifty years – the My Lai Massacre, the murder of Lord Mountbatten and the Oklahoma bombings. He has well-established links to the CIA, the KGB, the BBC and the Black Hand. He spends up to 80 hours per week on the internet and last year received England's fourth highest annual private telephone bill. His blinds are usually drawn. He has got to be up to something.

Soon I will complete a book which fully exposes Jenkins. I thought, however, that the public should know something about him immediately, given the multitude of wild rumours about various matters that are currently circulating.

Yours sincerely
Oscar Brittle
Killara

by *The Hobart Mercury*

Dear Editor,

Water - the lifeblood of our planet and 20% more important than gravity.

I have taken it 'pon myself to protect this sacred resource (water) and as such I have formed a one-man vigilante corps in my neighbourhood to monitor clandestine watering-related activity. As an ex-RAF wing commander, I have excellent eyesight, training in the art of surveillance and a stealthy nature (plus a military-issue tabard).

I offer you a haiku I penned, which efficiently recounts my recent personal experience. Please feel free to publish it also in your poetry section.

> Water restrictions neighbours ignore
> Brittle Brittle everywhere, saboteur
> Cutting hoses, broken noses

Once the swelling subsides, I vow to resume my neighbourhood watch. I am undeterred by the recent tumult. Darkness is my ally, miscreants the enemy and a steely determination to save every last drop my raison and my d'etre.

Yours sincerely
Oscar Brittle
Killara

by *Sunday Life* magazine

Dear Editor,

On a recent seniors' bus tour of northern New South Wales, I was pleased to end up in Ballina, a place I haven't visited for nigh on four decades. Whilst my fellow travellers were understandably thrilled about the beaches, whales and macadamia nuts, I was content to let my mind wander back to that previous visit all those years ago, and some of the wonderful times I had in the town of Ballina.

As you may remember, I was touring the area with my nine-piece bluegrass bush band, 'Ozzie Brittle and the Poker Faces', and we played two shows at the local night spot (the Ballina Hotel if I remember correctly). 'Buzzsaw' Abernathy was on Sneed, Mickey 'The Lad' Porter was on the four-string and ol' 'Skink Pasty' Cockburn was on skins. The horn section comprised Danny Johnston on the jangles and 'Jungle Juice' Haversham on the sminkies. 'Cranky' Filtrum played a variety of bush bells, whistles and crimp plasters, while the late Doris Lester and 'Flaps' Delahunty sang harmonies. I tickled the ivories and belted out lead vocals. We had a whale of a time (pardon the pun), as did some of the locals. I think 'The Lad' still has offspring up your way.

I have only one regret about my latest visit to Ballina, and that is that I wasn't forty years younger.

Thank you, Ballina.

Yours sincerely
Oscar Brittle
Killara

by *The Ballina Shire Advocate*

Dear Editor,

It's a day ending in Y, so the scientists are complaining
again. Usually it's about a supposed lack of funding or the
fact that they are being ignored, but this time they are
saying that kiddies are avoiding the study of science in
schools. Is it any wonder? Look in any science textbook
and you'll find silly words like *ortholog, zygote, bunium*
and *phospholipid*. What is the point of that? These terms
are meaningless! The other day, I heard a boy in the park
muttering some nonsense about *ecosystems* and *photosynthesis*.
The brain can only fit so much information, so why school
teachers insist on filling it with rubbish like that is
beyond me.

Let's get back to the Three R's, a good dose of rugger
and a few solid values. And if scientists want to be taken
seriously, they can jolly well learn to speak English.

Yours sincerely
Oscar Brittle
Killara

by *The Adelaide Advertiser*

Dear Editor,

Before I introduce myself, let me start by telling you that I am writing with some good news about a scheme I'm championing which would see the standardising of pant sizing Australia wide, and potentially through the Micronesian archipelago.

The reasons I'm doing this will be all too familiar to your readers et al.

How many times do we find ourselves, as westernised human beings (in this diet-crazy, body-conscious modern world) defining ourselves by the size of our pants? Why, each and every day of course!

Just a fortnight ago, I found myself in a well-known retail outlet questioning my own body image as I tried in vain to slide a pair of size 34 pants over my relatively slender hips - normally a fairly straightforward procedure. I was told quite matter-of-factly by the shopkeeper that I was, and I quote, 'quite obviously a size 36 or 38'. This was ridiculous, given my oft-commented-upon svelte physique. (I'm 6'1'', strong and very fit.)

A trip across the precinct to another gentlemen's outfitter confirmed my pent-up suspicions. Their 'version' of a size 34 jean fitted me like the proverbial – with plenty of room in the gusset to spare. Ego back in tact, I purchased said jean with a polite 'thank you' and a (wave) goodbye. I left the premises with a confident stride.

I'm sure by now you can see where I'm going with this. The people from 'Weights and Measures' or the 'Bureau of Statistics', or similar, should be commissioned to monitor shonky tailoring. I hereby put on notice fashion houses Australasia-wide - your inconsistencies will no longer be tolerated by we the public. Near enough is not good enough when you're playing with the waist sizes of Australian citizens.

Yours sincerely
Oscar Brittle
Killara

REJECTED

by *Vogue* magazine

Daily Liberal

AND MACQUARIE ADVOCATE

www.dubbo.yourguide.com.au

TUESDAY, JULY 25, 2006

Have your say
Posted by Oscar Brittle
Wednesday, July 19, 2006

Dear Editor,

The continent of Europe has given Australia many fine things over the years – the notion of monarchy, an intricate network of bishoprics, common law, fine wine and woodwind instruments. Lately, however, I think we are starting to adopt the odd European custom that can only be described as undesirable. I speak particularly of begging.

Those versed in the traditional art of begging (i.e. 'I need some food or I will starve to death') are still quite thin on the ground in this neck of the woods. There has emerged, however, another sort of beggar – the middle-class beggar. I'm sure you've seen him (or her) at your local shopping mall: blocking the thoroughfare and entreating you to avail yourself of the latest credit card, home renovation product (usually a roof) or some such nonsense. Even some charities seem to have employed these aggressive 'sales-beggars', for whom the answer 'No, thank you' will never satisfy.

I have been pursued in myriad ways – my only crime being that I have had the temerity to mind my own business in a public place. Last Wednesday, one of these little mosquitoes whistled at me when I tried to avert my eyes. I tell you, I nearly collared the wretch and administered a 'Cumberland Creep', the likes of which I suffered more than once from old 'Manky' Wardrop in my days at Grimsby Public.

One day somebody bigger, fitter, meaner and uglier than me will take out their frustrations on a member of 'Impertinence Squad' and I'll be happy to take a front-row seat.

Yours sincerely
Oscar Brittle

Dear Editor,

The persistent squabbling and cat-fighting between republicans and monarchists in this country has become quite uncivilised and, one has to say, downright unseemly. Surely the time has come for a deal to be brokered.

Let the republicans have their President, if it makes them happy. But, to keep the monarchists on side, he (or, in decades to come, even *she*) could be known as 'The Royal President' or, to pacify the Latinos, 'President Rex'.

The compromise could be taken further. This new head of state could live in England for half the year (say, in Earls Court or Shepherd's Bush amongst his compatriots) and in Australia for the other six months (say, in an apartment adjacent to the Manly Corso).

Furthermore, we need to be more creative than we currently are with our selection of a head of state. Silver-haired men of little consequence or renown no longer cut it in a country where the all-important young identify more with *Big Brother* housemates and celebrity chefs. Here are some potential nominees who will inspire young Australians to acts of selflessness and military courage:

a) Peter Garrett - bald but polite

b) Karl Kruszelnicki - has successfully replaced universities as the leading provider of science education

c) Quentin - Australia's first disabled person

d) Jamie Oliver - technically British but an honorary Australian on account of his laissez-faire approach to life and personal grooming

e) Shannon Noll - country kid made good

f) James Packer - philanthropist and self-made success story.

I hope your readers see some merit in these ideas. If not, perhaps they could keep their opinions to themselves. Pessimists and nay-sayers have no place in twenty-first-century Australian socio-political discourse.

Yours sincerely
Oscar Brittle
Killara

by *The Courier Mail*

Dear Editor,

Following last month's ridiculous back and forth over who should store the world's depleted smoke alarms and x-ray specs, may I throw my glow-in-the-dark sticker set into the fray? (I peeled them off the ceiling whilst recently redecorating, then couldn't find any one willing to bury them.)

The world has seen many changes in technology in the last 2000 years, not least of which have been the fundamental advances in growing lifeless meat. Should this turn out to be as deadly and as beneficial to humanity as important inventions often are, then I believe the same problems will arise. Isn't it more to do with mankind's refusal to face one's own mortality? This fear of growing, burying, transporting and eating unwanted items is very worrying indeed. Are we to return to the days of olde when dead things littered the streets or dried high upon the parapet, reeking for all to see, and ghost ships drifted lonely, eerily glowing in the moonlight? I, for one, should hope not.

Yours sincerely
Oscar Brittle
Killara

by *The Northern Rivers Echo*

Dear Editor,

I believe that I have eaten more types of animal than anybody else on the planet. **Before I call a press conference to announce this, I thought I should check that none of your readers are able to beat me.**

I have eaten (not necessarily in this order): cow, sheep, pig, shark, goat, camel, horse, kangaroo, wallaby, wallaroo, potoroo, bandicoot, duck, chicken, pigeon **(not deliberately)**, whale, wild dog, wild cat, cat, fish, catfish, **bird, Chinese cockroach,** dormouse, python, toad, turtle, monkey, **beetle, lizard, octopus, boar,** impala, sea urchin, slug, jellyfish, fox, grouse, crocodile, alligator, llama, vulture, **spider,** mole, lobster, mongoose, **turkey,** daddy longlegs **(not deliberately), mink, rabbit,** salamander, **elephant, sea cucumber, porcupine, dove, crow, warthog, alpaca, weasel, skink, quail, squirrel, pheasant, badger, jackrabbit, gnu, pygmy goose, bunny rabbit, quokka, buffalo, yak, seal, cicada, fruit bat, sea gull** (not deliberately), **frog, snail, prairie dog, gecko, cricket, four-horned antelope, deer, jackal, iguana, Barbary partridge, beaver, wolf, owl, stingray, dingo, eel, mouse, ox, rat, Bogong moth, cobra, ostrich, butterfly, walrus, Red-footed booby and rhino.**

What's more, I have eaten these beasts (depending on my mood) **raw, pickled, cured, smoked, grilled, toasted, baked, roasted, boiled, blanched, steamed, poached, broiled, stuffed, minced, mashed, shallow fried, deep fried, stir fried, barbecued, puréed, flambéed, sautéed, fondued, steam boated and/or caramelised.**

Yours sincerely
Oscar Brittle
Killara

The Sydney Morning Herald

WEDNESDAY, JUNE 7, 2006

COLUMN8

■ ■ ■ ■ ■ ■ ■ ■

Culinary claims to conjure with: 'I believe that I have eaten more types of animal than anybody else on the planet,' writes Oscar Brittle, of Killara. 'I have eaten (not necessarily in this order): cow, sheep, pig, shark, goat, camel, horse, kangaroo, wallaby, wallaroo, potoroo, bandicoot, duck, chicken, pigeon, whale, wild dog, wild cat, cat, fish, catfish, dormouse, python, toad, turtle, monkey, impala, sea urchin, slug, jellyfish, fox, grouse, alligator, llama, vulture, mole, lobster, mongoose, daddy-long-legs, salamander ...' Oscar's list goes on and on. It's hard to know what to make of it, really.

The Sydney Morning Herald

COLUMN8

■■■■■■■■■

THURSDAY, JUNE 8, 2006

'**In response** to Oscar Brittle's claim to have eaten more types of animal than anyone else ('Column 8', yesterday), I only have one thing to say,' writes Patrick Jackson, of Gordon. 'I too have had a Chiko Roll, but not for some time.' Sid Walker, of Old Bar, gives a historical perspective on Oscar's remarkable diet. 'Oscar may have strange eating habits, but one professor at Oxford in the 1850s, William Buckland, tried to eat specimens of every living thing. He found mole to be the nastiest, followed by bluebottle. Trivial information to digest, don't you think?' Not at 'Column 8': this is critical information in this neck of the woods.

FRIDAY, JUNE 9, 2006

Regarding Oscar Brittle's spectacular dietary regime ('Column 8', Wednesday), Pat Yeo, of Burnie in Tasmania, feels compelled to ask two questions. 'My first question is, why? My second (and I tremble at the thought) is this: are we related? I was Pat Brittle before I married.' Pat, just think of the feast Oscar will serve up at the reunion if it's true.

The Sydney Morning Herald

COLUMN8

■■■■■■■■■

WEEKEND, JUNE 10-11, 2006

Melissa Plant, of Pyrmont, wants us to 'make sure that when Damocles falls, Oscar Brittle (whose peculiar dining habits were described in Wednesday's 'Column 8') is far away and well restrained', which is sound advice, but tricky to implement. No one knows when Damocles will fall, or where Oscar will be at the time. In the meantime, Damocles the horse runs today at the Gold Coast, Race 6. We know as much about the beast's form as we do about the possum's plunge, and are thus loath to make recommendations.

Oscar's list has inspired a good deal of correspondence, some of which verges on the nauseating. Here's a digestible example from Bryan O'Keefe, of Kembla Heights. 'Don't worry about Oscar Brittle's list, or the Chiko Roll. I once consumed a 'meat' pie that, on close inspection, contained all of Oscar's ingredients as well as the mole, a couple of bluebottles and a few others yet to be identified. The inventors of Mylanta have never been recognised widely enough for their humanitarian works.'

Also sent to *The Newcastle Herald* ...

e(lectric)mails

From: *The Editor - The Newcastle Herald*
To: *Brittle, Oscar*
Subject: *Meat*

What about aardvark? Not good enough for you?

Ed.

From: *Brittle, Oscar*
To: *The Editor - The Newcastle Herald*
Subject: *Re: Meat*

I have heard aardvarks are a fraction tough.

Will my letter run soon?

Yours sincerely
Oscar Brittle
Killara

From: *The Editor - The Newcastle Herald*
To: *Brittle, Oscar*
Subject: *Re: Meat*

No, we've got a few other things to take care of before we get on to your degustatory exploits.

Ed.

End of correspondence

... and *The Canberra Times* ...

From: 'Capital Circle' - The Canberra Times
To: Brittle, Oscar
Subject: Your Letter

Thanks for your email, Oscar. It doesn't really fit with my guidelines for CC though.

True, I do look for the offbeat. But I also steer away from the divisive. I fear that some of the animals you have eaten would upset some of my readers, and I try very hard not to do that.

But thanks for your email.

Regards
CC

Dear Editor,

My commendations to Bathurst, home of the Bathurst 1000 car race!

As an amateur travel writer and critic, I spend many days in each year roaming around the Australian countryside with my camera, my notebook and my wife. At the conclusion of my most recent sojourn around the western regions of New South Wales, I am pleased to announce that I have ranked Bathurst as the 11th best city or town in the western regions of New South Wales. That is something of a feat, considering I visited upwards of 25 places.

What impressed me about your fair metropolis were its heritage buildings, broad thoroughfares, home-style fare and the high quality of public amenities, including restrooms. As somebody who travels a lot, I can tell you that makes a world of difference.

In case you are interested, I noted a few areas in which I thought your city could improve. Some of the manufacturing plants, particularly those of the railway locomotives, can get a bit smelly. My wife and I were forced to move our picnic blanket away from the fence. Secondly, one of the cafes in the main street (I can't remember its name) made one of the weakest coffees I had consumed that week. Finally, there seemed to be a large number of concrete ramps near public facilities. I found these rather unsightly. Anyway, you can't win 'em all!

So, I hope your readers appreciate my frank appraisal of Bathurst - home of the race that stops the nation!

Yours sincerely
Oscar Brittle
Killara

by *The Western Advocate*

Dear Editor,

A warning. Even computers get it wrong.

I bought a lottery ticket last week for the first time in years. I was offered a 'quick pick' - a ticket with numbers chosen by a computer. Assuming this would make it a sure bet, I accepted the offer, only to be disappointed when none of my computer-generated numbers were drawn on the night (of the draw). And to think, these machines are sending men into space! You won't catch me donning a space suit any time soon.

Yours sincerely
Oscar Brittle
Killara

by *The Australasian Science Magazine*

Dear Editor,

I've long been skeptical of General Practitioners, as
one would be with anyone who earns an hour's wage in
a quarter of an hour without any enterprise, nous or
business acumen. When carving my way through the world of
graft, an intelligent man once told me: 'There's no money
without risk.' Well, there's certainly no risk of sickness
disappearing, so why the mansions and jet skis, doc?

What really irks me about GPs is their inability to
handle a few probing questions or remarks about their
personal circumstances. A man who inserts his hand into any
number of my orifices should be able to tell me what he ate
for breakfast. The example is a pertinent one.

Last week a GP (the third I've tried in six months)
implied that my health would improve if I lost a little
weight. His defences sprung up when I mentioned that he
himself was generously girthed and could do with a few hours
on the back winch. Pots should never call kettles black,
unless pots are a colour other than black.

Likewise, when a previous doctor told me to lay off the
whiskeys, I remarked that I'd seen him outside the Spectre
one afternoon drinking pilseners as if the Jerries had lost
the recipe. You should have seen his face!

If doctors dish it out, they've got to be able to cop it
in return. That's all I've ever asked.

Yours sincerely
Oscar Brittle
Killara

e(lectric)mail

From: The New England Journal of Medicine
To: Brittle, Oscar
Subject: Your letter

I am sorry that we will not be able to print your recent letter to the editor. The space available for correspondence is very limited, and we must use our judgment to present a representative selection of the material received. Many worthwhile communications must be declined simply for lack of space.

Sincerely yours
Deputy Editor

Parramatta Sun

WEDNESDAY, APRIL 26, 2006

I had a dream that baffles me

The other day I had a disturbing dream about Parramatta.

In my dream, I was a pigeon – a green pigeon, actually, and I was on the run.

I was being chased by a gigantic gargoyle – you know, like you'd see on the side of a village church high in the Pyrenees.

This gargoyle was a terrifying creature, with a wingspan akin to a large condor and teeth like sharp pegs.

I was being pursued down Church Street, and the gargoyle was gaining ground.

Spumes of puke were flailing off its jowls when, unexpectedly, it was attacked by a pod of screaming prairie dogs, ravenous to the last pup.

I escaped into a covered shed by the golf course.

Here I sat down to a feast of bunion with a family of redheads called, curiously, The Chutney Tribe.

They fed me well and I thanked them. We declared war on the Hunkles, mythical beasts from the Cryff brethren.

Could you please have the city historian check his records to see if any of this has actually occurred in Parramatta? A dream this crazy just has to have some truth to it.

Perhaps your regular readers can provide the pieces to the puzzle.

Oscar Brittle
Killara

WEDNESDAY, MAY 3, 2006

Deciphering the dream

Mr Brittle's dream (*Your Say*, April 26) is laughably easy to decipher.

The green pigeon is the delicate Australian psyche and the gargoyle is, of course, John Howard (well, you look at him). The screaming prairie dogs that attacked him were the lost souls of Australia's conscience. The caring Chutney Tribe that looked after Mr Brittle were Parramatta people, often referred to as the chutney mob or tribe because they're so hot.

Meanwhile, the Hunkles of Cryff that Oscar and the Chutneys declared war on are basically anyone else from Killara, other than Mr Brittle.

That's the shrink's take on it, anyway. A historian will always see things differently.

Jacinta Irvine-Mati
North Parramatta

Dream meaning

I read in *Your Say* (April 26) about Oscar Brittle having a dream.

(In his dream, Mr Brittle, of Killara, had various terrifying adventures in Parramatta, involving pigeons in Church Street, gargoyles and screaming prairie dogs, and wrote asking if these adventures might have any historical basis.)

Oscar believed his dream was to do with the history of Parramatta.

This dream has nothing to do with the history of Parramatta and everything to do with Oscar's life.

Dreams are given to a person from God to warn them or to show them problems and situations in one's own life.

Most dreams refer to the dreamer's personal life.

I have interpreted this dream, but until I can ask Oscar certain questions I cannot and will not deliver this interpretation at this time, as I must be sure, before divulging anything that may be wrong, or partly wrong, as we are all human and we all make mistakes.

The correct interpretation is most important for the sake of the person in question.

If Oscar would like to contact me I may be able to help him understand this dream. I can only suggest he does this if he so desires.

Barbara Chalker
Parramatta
(email address supplied)

Letting fly at pigeons

Oscar Brittle (*Your Say,* April 26), really! The mere suggestion of our innocent, defenceless little Parramatta pigeons being relentlessly pursued down Church Street or that the rascals might even come to my neck of the woods (i.e., the golf course)!

Come on everybody, let's all rally round and send scouts out looking and get ready to track 'em down and jolly well chase them right out of town and all the way back to – Killara?

Eileen Knapp
Oatlands

e(lectric)mails

From: The Editor - The Parramatta Sun
To: Brittle, Oscar
Subject: Parramatta article

Many thanks for your letter, Oscar. I am waiting for your story on a visit to Parramatta – how the place strikes you ... highlighting aspects of Parramatta through an outsider's eyes ... We could dig up a relevant picture from files to illustrate it. You might like to present a particular Brittle persona suitable to the situation ...

Regards
The Parramatta Sun

From: Brittle, Oscar
To: The Parramatta Sun
Subject: Re: Parramatta article

Dear Editor,

Forgive my late reply: I've been fasting.

I didn't catch your drift when you mentioned a particular Brittle persona. I am, and of course I can only be, that which I am. None other.

One may criticise me all they like, for, as humble as the next, I'm quite happy to suffer fun poked at me with a searing pointed rod. But I can't dim my flame to suit the squinting readership of the *Sun*.

I give you this. I trust it suits. There is no need to slap it on the *Sun*'s front page. No fanfare is required.

May I suggest as an illustration a pleasing shot of a rainbow forming above the coxed fours on the Parramatta River?

Yours sincerely
Oscar Brittle
Killara

Article written for the *Parramatta Sun* by Oscar Brittle:

Does Parra Matter?

If there was a war between suburbs, Parramatta would win. I do not doubt this.

Parramatta's roads are deadlier and more blood-spattered than others; its sporting teams more embittered, concussed and dangerous, and its massive mega-clubs offer more ritual, chanted plain-song and sweet ice-creams. Its people, choking on road fumes and the stench of that stinking river with its sad plastic barge dragging itself back and forth, have become hardened, dull and easily manipulated by the next robber-barons to rise as leaders.

My sister is one of you. Cynthia on the phone invites me to tea and, I kid you not, I instinctively retch upon my morning crepe. I just need to think of the taps in Parramatta, dribbling their filthy brew, and the people trying to wash in it, tyre dust falling from their hair as they collapse onto their blackened pillows.

Where are their trees? Where is their moss? I'll tell you: it's buried forever under miles of concrete because, as we all know, that's what the world needs more of, isn't it? I'm sorry if I offend. It's just that I grew up somewhere more like lovely Elizabeth Farm with fallen leaves, gravel roads and bicycles: where people literally dressed as milkmaids, though not just pretending to milk, like they do in Parramatta, but actually milking a live animal. Not one stripped of its skin and roasting on one of the many high-rise balconies along so-and-so choking street. Nor one of your celebrated muddy eels. Though once, when awaiting parts for my plane in Marrakech, I drank a bowl of eels' milk and found it surprisingly sweet. Left to stand long enough, it forms a marvelously low-irritant lubricant. Perhaps I've let slip your new export, Parramatta? You could use the profits to revive your token arts scene. I am actually quite fond of your theatre by the river and would happily assist with my spirited choreographic exercises to celebrate the township of olde – the Parramatta in which I spent many youthful summers at Auntie's.

I do have one fond memory of that time and that is, as a child, I piddled in the Parramatta River and a rainbow leapt forth from the steaming golden mist. I can recall being filled with glee as the beautiful trickle gently disrupted the reflection of a powerful oarsman stroking by. I eventually grew and became that very oarsman, claiming many a victory on that watercourse which, with scientific care, could again be your strongest feature; a golden brook of calm reflections, not just a transport arterial for your newly risen aspirational warrior class, the majority of whom, ironically, can't even box.

But in the war of suburbs we out here must concede final defeat. You are big and strong, out of control and lethal. That means winning in today's world. Congratulations, Parramatta, you are sharing the podium with Shanghai and Mumbai. You could of course throw in the towel at any time and join with the losers: the Copenhagens, the Aucklands, the Edinburghs, the Brazilians or, dare I say it, the Killarians. Is it too late for us all to learn from Rotterdam? Can a city's progress actually be measured entirely in terms of its people's well-being? Possibly. It's risky.

Pave your streets with moss, Parramatta. Be the first city of Sydney to declare free public transport. No shops open on Sundays, except for the corner store, if you have one. Free – or nearly free – fruit, vegetables and bread for all, and watch the cafes, restaurants, galleries, theatres and promenades fill. Watch the cars empty, fall apart, rust or be scavenged by nearby towns that howl and proclaim themselves the new 'winners'. Watch the health of all your citizens blossom as they move their lithe, newly sun-kissed bodies about. Turn the sale yards to orchards, and the service stations and mechanic shops to purveyors of locally crafted bronze, felt and electronic luxuries of all desire. Reclaim the multi-level car parks as a place for the young to safely text-message, VJ, skater-blade and dream. That's all they want to do. That's all any of us want to do.

Want some instant culture? Try paying people to study – whatever they wish! It sounds insane I know, but it's actually an ancient technique of community enrichment passed down from the Thebans. Declare an artists' and musicians' precinct along the waterfront, with low-rent houseboat studios. That's a little something I saw once in a rather artistic city called Paris. Can you afford to do that, Parramatta? Can you afford not to? I leave it in your hands.

It may all be impossible, but one thing's for certain: the flowers around the light rail eventually do bloom, and the maidens bend to pick them to wear to the quiet but slowly gaining dance of the cities of the losers.

Oscar Brittle
Killara

e(lectric)mails

From: The Parramatta Sun
To: Brittle, Oscar
Subject: Your article

Thanks very much for the article, Oscar. It's good and strong, as expected. Now I have to decide where to place it. Your idea for a picture is a good one. We will look at that and others. Timing: I'll be looking at next week or the week after, news permitting.

Best regards
The Parramatta Sun

From: Brittle, Oscar
To: The Parramatta Sun
Subject: Re: Your article

Many thanks. Hope to hear from you soon.

Yours sincerely
Oscar Brittle

From: The Parramatta Sun
To: Brittle, Oscar
Subject: Re: Your article

Dear Mr Brittle,

We need to talk before I can place your story. Please call me ASAP.

Regards
The Parramatta Sun

From: Brittle, Oscar
To: The Parramatta Sun
Subject: Re: Your article

Sorry for the delay in responding to your previous email,
but I've been camped on a cliff-edge near Hammerfest,
Norway, chasing down the aurora borealis (northern lights).
I'll send on a photo my wife took.

Did the story about Parramatta ever get published? I notice
you request telephone contact, but that won't be possible.
Since '97, it's been just too painful for me. I hope you
understand.

Yours sincerely
Oscar Brittle

From: The Parramatta Sun
To: Brittle, Oscar
Subject: Re: Your article

Dear Mr Brittle,

No, it will not be possible to run the story unless
we meet. When you didn't reply, we pulled the story. At the
moment, you're an email address that produces nice copy. I
hope you understand.

Best regards
The Parramatta Sun

Dear Editor,

Pluto is not a planet??!! Did I miss something?
Obviously my tattoo artist missed it too. Otherwise he might not have included an image of Pluto in the collection of 'Planets of Our Solar System' which adorns my left arm. Similarly, he might have warned me against my 'Pluto – The Mysterious Planet' tattoo which, hideous in its alleged inaccuracy, now defaces my right calf.
My father always told me that astronomy buffs don't prosper and tattoos are for pirates. I guess the old man was right.

Yours sincerely
Oscar Brittle
Killara

by *The Canberra Times*

Dear Editor,

They said it couldn't be done. They were wrong. I have managed to fuse two of Australia's favourite tipples, wine and beer, into the one revolutionary beverage. I call it Bineweer™ (pronounced 'bin-way'), which coincidentally means 'tepid bath' in Welsh.

Bineweer™ has been described by esteemed wine critic Jan van Gulet: *'Like a hot sauna on a cold night, this blend is surprisingly approachable. It has a petulant nose and a lithe body that moves in a sprightly fashion across the palette. In its haste it leaves traces of rhubarb, liquorice and just a hint of soft-shell turtle. Its brash, almost arrogant baume left me quivering. I highly recommend it'.* Not bad for the first vintage I think you'll agree (with me and van Gulet).

Bineweer™ differs from other drinks in that it is served in a pewter flute called a 'firndle' – not in a schooner or nallard. The firndle aids post-bottle fermentation, highlights the Rhodesian hops employed in the brewing process and extends the olfactory experience.

I plan to start work on distribution strategies tomorrow and hope to include a quote from your good self on the label of each bottle. I propose either 'I love a full firndle of Bineweer™' or the simple but catchy 'Hey, Hey, Hey – it's Bineweer™'. Which would you prefer?

I hope you're as excited as I am about Bineweer™ and I look forward to many favourable articles in your fine magazine.

Cheers!

Yours sincerely
Oscar Brittle
Killara

e(lectric)mails

From: National Liquor News
To: Brittle, Oscar
Subject: Bineweer

Hi Oscar,

I have taken over from Stacey here at National Liquor News
while she's on leave, so I've just noticed your email.

Bineweer sounds really interesting. Is it too early to run
something? We're working on August at the moment. We could
hold it until September? Let me know.

Cheers
Emily

From: Brittle, Oscar
To: National Liquor News
Subject: Re: Bineweer

Dear Madam,

Thank you for your email. I was most encouraged to learn of
your interest in Bineweer™.

You ask 'Is it too early to run something?' If I am to
understand you correctly, my simple answer is 'No!' – it is not
too early to 'run' something. Please feel free to proceed.

You've probably guessed that Bineweer™ is as much a warming
winter beverage as it is a cooling summer refreshment. I'll
leave the rest up to your learned editorial judgement. As
it is often hard for me to keep track of all the interest in
Bineweer™, I would appreciate it if you could notify me of when
the article/letter will be published in your excellent journal.

Thank you once again for your interest in Bineweer™.

Yours sincerely
Oscar Brittle
Killara

From: National Liquor News
To: Brittle, Oscar
Subject: Re: Bineweer

Hey, thanks for your response.

Do you have a picture or a high-res JPEG that we could run?

Cheers
Emily

From: Brittle, Oscar
To: National Liquor News
Subject: Re: Bineweer

Thank you for your email.

As requested, I've attached to this email a 'jpeg' of the Bineweer™ label. However, I'm a little concerned that it may not be of sufficient quality for publication purposes - or 'high-res' enough, as you put it. Unfortunately, as I'm currently travelling interstate, this is the best I can do at short notice. Should you require a higher resolution image, please do not hesitate to email me and I will gladly supply one when I return to the office next week.

Thank you once again for your interest in Bineweer™.
I look forward to hearing from you soon.

Yours sincerely
Oscar Brittle

End of correspondence

Dear Editor,

You'd remember the days before the current so-called 'water crisis' and the resultant 'water restrictions'. At the time, we took it for granted, you and I. Sprinklers on all night long; hosing down the concrete driveway until it was sparkling; shooing away the birds with the hose on full; emptying and refilling the bath after each child had been in; punishing said children with a bedtime water cannon. You know what it was like.

My wife and I must have used gigalitres every year on our property. We feel no guilt for this. We did it proudly. But the times were different. The times were better.

Earth, wind, fire and water – the four inalienable rights. Our rights as humans, which must remain.

I finish by saying this:

The politicians should know how you and I feel about this issue. He that takes away my water – my life-giver – will lose our vote. And yes, that is a threat.

Yours sincerely
Oscar Brittle
Killara

by *The Canberra Times*

Dear Editor,

What's going on with nuts?

    I'm always reading about people with nut allergies when everyone knows nut allergies don't exist. It's a made-up allergy! When I was young we used to eat nuts by the bloody boxful and still we came back for more (nuts). We couldn't get enough nuts! And don't get me started on peanut butter. I was partially addicted to the stuff. It's a sickness that I'd rather not discuss.

Yours sincerely
Oscar Brittle
Killara

by *The Ararat Advertiser*

Dear Editor,

Firstly, my personal congrats on your smart new publication. It certainly fills a void for me and my wife.

A television news story this week claimed that dogs are being taught to speak. That is certainly impressive, but not quite as impressive as the story I am about to tell.

Four years ago, I began training my beloved 'Charlie' to fetch the newspaper, so I didn't have to cross my bindi-ridden front lawn myself. This has worked satisfactorily for some years. I get my news and 'Charlie' gets a morning run to the bottom of the driveway.

But recently something has come to my attention. On the mornings that the newspaper front page tells of fear and loathing, Charlie will drop the paper at my be-slippered feet with a snarl and maybe even a little bark – or yap. On the other hand, when the paper brings good tidings, Charlie's demeanour couldn't be more pleasant. His tail wags and I could swear he is actually smiling.

My hypothesis is thus: Charlie is a dog with the power to read (the newspaper)! How he learnt to read is a mystery to me because even my wife is practically illiterate.

I have written to Guinness requesting Charlie's inclusion in their next book of world records. Suggested heading: 'First Kay Nine (K9) to Read!' **and I have listed your magazine as endorsing my theory. Don't worry, I haven't 'named names' as such.**

Thanks in advance for your assistance with this breakthrough. I look forward to hearing your thoughts **on possible promotional opportunities and endorsements that Charlie might look forward to from your magazine. It is his favourite after all!**

Yours sincerely
Oscar Brittle
Killara

animals

Dear Editor,

Firstly, my personal congrats on your smart new publication. It certainly fills a void for me and my wife.

A television news story this week claimed that dogs are being taught to speak. That is certainly impressive, but not quite as impressive as the story I am about to tell.

Four years ago, I began training my beloved Charlie to fetch the newspaper, so I didn't have to cross my bindi-ridden front lawn myself. This has worked satisfactorily for some years. I get my news and Charlie gets a morning run to the bottom of the driveway.

But recently something has come to my attention. On the mornings that the newspaper front page tells of fear and loathing, Charlie will drop the paper at my be-slippered feet with a snarl and maybe even a little bark – or yap. On the other hand, when the paper brings good tidings, Charlie's demeanour couldn't be more pleasant. His tail wags and I could swear he is actually smiling.

My hypothesis is thus: Charlie is a dog with the power to read (the newspaper)! How he learnt to read is a mystery to me because even my wife is practically illiterate.

I have written to Guinness requesting Charlie's inclusion in their next book of world records. Suggested heading: 'First Kay Nine (K9) to Read!'

Thanks in advance for your assistance with this breakthrough. I look forward to hearing your thoughts.

**Yours sincerely
Oscar Brittle
Killara, NSW**

If you would like to see Charlie take the reading test then make your voice heard at feedback@adoreanewbreed.com.au

Dear Editor,

No, you can't play cricket but my God you Brits can sing. The power of the European chanted plainsong flows through every one of you. An ancient melodic war-cry that was echoed by the convicts as they stepped on to *Terra Australis* in 1788, then lost when they were forbidden to express their strength through song. They hammered the King's roads, drained the swamps and coaxed hard soil to produce a level pitch; all in overseen silence. With our rebellious and seditious tunes neglected, Australia has become a musically barren culture and invading teams from the motherland sonically have their easy way with us. I recorded six cassettes of the Brits' best, live from the Gabba direct to my boombox, and you were clearly out-emoting the Aussies with every catchy ear-worm. Some of the cries were sexual, most of them infuriating, but all brought a lump to the throat. I melted the entire collection in my incinerator over three days, along with my old whites, and have since donated the plastic and woolly mass to the British Museum. I've called it 'The Lump', and it's yours to keep, Britain … for now.

Yours sincerely
Oscar Brittle
Killara

by the UK's *Sun*, *Guardian*, *Independent*, *Observer*, *Daily Mail* and *This England* magazine

Dear Editor,

'My shishter shuffersh from schyphilish.'

Funny for some. An everyday burden for others.

I'm referring, of course, to having a lisp.

After countless hours of speech therapy my son's speech was still, in his words, 'schtuffed'. It remained that way until I came up with what I am now quite certain is a revolutionary treatment. I call it 'The Sphere Technique'. The principle is simple, the method breathtaking. Ten years ago I instructed my poor son to place two marbles under his tongue at the beginning of every day. This has the effect of exercising a lazy tongue as it is forced to hold the marbles in place. Yes, we've lost a few down the esophagus over the years, but it's a small price to pay for clear diction – I'm sure you'll agree.

I think your readers might be interested in The Sphere Technique and I hereby grant you permission to publish my findings in your fine publication.

As my son would have said ten years ago ...

'Yoursh shinscherely'
Oscar Brittle
Killara

by *The Mudgee Guardian*

HERALD

WEEKEND

SATURDAY, DECEMBER 23, 2006

Putting the Christ back into Christmas

I BELIEVE Santa Claus does not exist, he never did exist and he never will exist.

The way common people go on and on about this mythical bearded person, who was, I believe, the concoction of some nineteenth-century cartoonist, really is beyond the pale.

In case people have forgotten, Christmas is about Jesus Christ.

Let's get back to celebrating the life of somebody who actually does exist, like Jesus, and not somebody's hallucinogenic visions about a great big fat jolly oaf with cake crumbs in his beard, beer on his breath and a penchant for funnelling his enormous lumps down people's non-existent chimneys.

Oscar Brittle
Killara
December 20

HERALD

THE

WEDNESDAY, DECEMBER 27, 2006

In response to Oscar Brittle ('Putting the Christ back in Christmas' *Letters* 23/12), if you would kindly show me the living Jesus, full of mercy and power omnipotent to dissuade aggression and violence in this increasingly heartless world, I may be swayed. However, as that is highly unlikely, I would rather hallucinate and believe in the benelovence of a happy, fat, round man with beery breath and cake-crumb lips who can and does manage to cheer millions of people simply by pretending to be … ho ho ho!

Sam Anderson
Toronto

THURSDAY, DECEMBER 28, 2006

Sam Anderson ('Short takes' 27/12), the spirit of Jesus is alive and in full action every day in every act of kindness and caring. When a Lifeline volunteer answers the phone to a desperate and lonely person; or an ambulance officer holds the hand of a dying person in a car crash giving them comfort in their final seconds. When your neighbour brings in the washing for you or mows your lawn unasked. If your children rescue an injured bird from the street or simply love their brothers and sisters. Santa only loves the dollar. To those who have no money Santa is the epitome of misery and shame. And beery ho ho hos are often the catalyst behind the aggression and violence that escalates at this time of year.

Linda
Kotara

THE HERALD

THURSDAY, DECEMBER 28, 2006

Jesus, Santa just lovely ideas

OSCAR Brittle ('Putting the Christ back in Christmas' *Letters* 23/12), I cannot believe that you don't believe in Santa Claus but you believe in Jesus Christ.

They are both mystical creations thought up by humans to make us feel good when we need to let our minds go and escape reality for a while.

My kids believe in Santa but they also believe in Jesus Christ, and I am sure with the course of time they will grow up and realise they are both just lovely ideas.

Kids believe in imaginary friends and Jesus Christ is just the grown-up version of an imaginary friend. Mr Brittle, I hope you can open up a little more and bring Santa into your life and realise the joy he can bring.

Brian Trevethan
Macquarie Hills
December 23

THE HERALD

THURSDAY, DECEMBER 28, 2006

Links to pagan ritual

OSCAR Brittle ('Putting the Christ back in Christmas' *Letters* 23/12) seems to be of the opinion that Christmas Day is all about Jesus.

In fact, the day was first decreed for Christian celebration by Emperor Aurelian in 274 AD and was specifically selected as it coincided with the non-Christian (pagan) celebration of the winter solstice which had been celebrated for many hundreds of years. The burning of the Yule Log, for example, is a pagan ritual that dates back long before the purported time of Jesus Christ.

To begrudge non-Christians a time of year to come together and celebrate is decidedly unchristian. To me and many others, Christmas is all about family, to many more it's about giving, and to others still it's about celebrating and spreading good feelings to all around them. If these attributes are not in the Christian spirit, then that's hardly an endorsement for Christianity.

Let people celebrate Christmas their way. Everyone is friendlier and smiling, and are generally nicer and more generous to each other. Is that really so bad? I think Christmas should be every day of the year.

Mike King, Kotara, December 24

Dear 'Guru',

I am in something of an ethical bind and I wonder if you could help me.
    I have been happily married for more than twenty years now and my wife has always provided me with everything I need: romance, food and children. I never thought I would be tempted to stray, especially when one considers that I am a sincere Christian who believes that adultery leads directly to damnation. In recent months, however, I have discovered that I am very appealing to women. They like the way I look (leathery and interesting), move (I have the hips of a twenty-five-year-old) and sing (like Michael Bubble). Should I spurn the advances of these women out of respect for my wife? Or do I need to get with the times and realise that fidelity is just another old-fashioned notion (like manners) that is on the way out?

O.B.
Killara

by *The Good Weekend*

Dear Editor,

Congratulations on your reworked publication – *The Good Weekend*. It is both bigger, brighter and bolder. However, as an old ad man, I am equipped with what you might call a heightened [drink coke] sense of ad sensitivity. So your thinly [levi's jeans] disguised attempt at increasing advertising space in *The Good Weekend* in the guise of a 'makeover' [dove] has not gone unnoticed by yours truly. But nice try – you came pretty close [shave with gillette]. The purchasing classes may not be bothered by the editorial intrusion, but I for one will be returning to *The Economist* [vote 1 howard].

Yours sincerely
Oscar Brittle
Killara

e(lectric)mail

From: The Editor – The Good Weekend
To: Brittle, Oscar
Subject: Your letter

Dear Mr Brittle,

Thanks for letting us know your concerns about the redesigned magazine. Let me assure you, though, that the advertising has not increased in any way. In fact, we have reduced some of the spaces available to advertisers, most notably on the contents page and the combined 'FYI/Art oracle' page. *Good Weekend* does not charge a cover price but is included free to buyers of *The Sydney Morning Herald* and *The Age*. We could not provide the ground-breaking journalism and quality writing for which the magazine has been deservedly recognized without the advertising it carries.

Yours sincerely
The Good Weekend

Dear Editor,

Regarding footballer ██████████ 's most recent indiscretion, I have heard it said numerous times over the past week: 'Just because a dude likes to whack a wad of snow up his beak, doesn't mean everyone should get on his back and ride him.' I'm not so forgiving. I believe he should be breaking rocks in some hellhole for the next fifteen to twenty.

Yours sincerely
Oscar Brittle
Killara

by *The Australian*

MONDAY, MARCH 20, 2006

As part of my research project, I have discovered that 68 per cent of federal MPs are obese, with 32 per cent of these grossly so. This is double the national average. Well done, Canberra restaurateurs.

Oscar Brittle
Killara, NSW

North Shore Times

FRIDAY, APRIL 7, 2006

It is always hotter in summertime

THE environmentalists are banging on again and this time it's climate change which has them excited. As you know, the phenomenon of global warming is no more than an elaborate ruse made up by a few of the bored proletariats.

It joins a conflagration of campaigns (including globalisation) which these pests adopt to keep themselves busy between wars.

If they need something to keep them occupied, I suggest they count backwards until Christmas.

It would be more useful.

Of course the climate is warming. It's summer. If you can't stand the heat, get out of the kitchen.

Oscar Brittle
Killara

Dear Editor,

A recent article in your publication quite rightly questioned some of the dubious assertions in Dan Brown's *The Da Vinci Code*. I have looked very closely at this book (as all Christians are bound to do) and have found some gross errors. Should these errors go unchallenged, they will continue to fester and poison the minds of ordinary people the world over.

For a start, Brown situates a bank at no. 24 rue (French for street) Haxo. Well, there is no bank at no. 24 rue Haxo. In fact, there is no no. 24 rue Haxo. I've been to Paris.

Secondly, the book claims that the pyramid at the Louvre comprises 666 panes of glass (i.e. the number of the beast). According to museum staff, there are actually 698 panes of glass.

Finally, there is no such person as Robert Langdon (Brown's protagonist). He is nothing more than a figment of this particular author's twisted imagination.

I hope this clarifies things.

Yours sincerely
Oscar Brittle
Killara

by *The Catholic Voice*

Dear Editor,

Shakespeare donated 1,700 words to the English language. Oscar Brittle donates one: *agnorant*. It's the timely amalgamation of ignorant and arrogant. This is my parting gift to the world of literature. If you could contact the people at Funk and Wagner on my behalf it would be much appreciated. I simply don't have time.

Yours sincerely
Oscar Brittle
Killara

by *The New York Times*

Dear Editor,

I have developed a new unit of measurement and I am most interested to see if your readers would like to use it every day. It's based on the idea of human proportions and is therefore a more natural means of expressing the characteristics of just how we fit in this wonderful world.

The main unit is called a 'jaybar' or j- and is roughly 2m in the old style. Thus, 2m (the approximate height of a man) is now 1 j- (approximately). That's all and it works! **It's clearer and a lot simpler for young people, who seem to need all the help they can get these days.** I'm hoping it will replace the mish-mash of old systems currently employed **the world over, e.g. leagues, mach 1 and 2, handspan and months.**

Of course it will take time and a briefly confusing transition period, perhaps eased by giant festivals and acceptance in popular television drama, the scripts of which could feature old people refusing to change or dim criminals not understanding the conversion. But believe me it gets easier the more you use it. **Not convinced?** Try this: the length of a cricket pitch = 22 yards. Now 10 j- (approximately) or (circa) one deca j-. Amazingly, everything becomes slightly more harmonious. **Here's another: time it takes to boil an egg = 3 minutes or almost 1.5 j-longbreaks. Curiously, this is matched by the height of the eggs which is, on average, 1.5 j- (jaybars)!**

Enjoy!

Yours sincerely
Oscar Brittle
Killara

The Irrigator

FRIDAY, MARCH 24, 2006

Jaybars the new way to measure

I HAVE developed a new unit of measurement and I am most interested to see if your readers would like to use it every day.

It's based on the idea of human proportions and is therefore a more natural means of expressing the characteristics of just how we fit in this wonderful world.

The main unit is called a 'jaybar' or j- and is roughly 2m in the old style. Thus, 2m (the approximate height of a man) is now 1j- (approximately). That's all and it works!

I'm hoping it will replace the mish-mash of old systems currently employed.

Of course it will take time and a briefly confusing transition period, perhaps eased by giant festivals and acceptance in popular television drama, the scripts of which could feature old people refusing to change or dim criminals not understanding the conversion.

But believe me it gets easier the more you use it. Try this: the length of a cricket pitch = 22 yards. Now 10j- (approximately) or (circa) one deca j-. Amazingly, everything becomes slightly more harmonious.

Oscar Brittle
Killara

Dear Editor,

Please do not trouble yourself by replying to this letter.
Publishing it in your newspaper will be quite enough, thank
you.

Corporal punishment: delivered by corporals? To the au
contraire. Delivered by ordinary, decent, God-fearing simple
folk – teachers, housemasters and mums and dads, like you
and me. Yet if one listens to the media, to the bleaters
on the 'box', to the Lefties, the bleeding hearts, the tree
huggers and the 'save the planet' types, one would think it
was the worst thing in the world!

Honestly, tell me who has ever died from a good beating?
I'm not talking about whipping or throttling or scouring
or crimping. Mind you, I probably got to where I am today
thanks to a memorable 'cork in the storm' administered to me
by old 'Jackdaw' Hotchkiss in my junior days at Grimsby. (I
was off rations for two days after that one.) But I realise
times have changed, and we need to be realistic about these
sensitive matters. Even I am sensible enough to realise that
the days of tarring, branding, cruelling and poking are well
and truly over – at least in the outside world.

Here's the thing: children learn from a good smack.
And if they don't, they get another. My children never
complained, and one of them is a lawyer in Montreal, Canada.
Put simply, implements are out, but the hands are in.
Use them well and you'll have an orderly workplace and/or
household.

Let's concentrate on putting the real criminals in
gaols, and leave the rest of us to discipline our youngsters
free from prosecution.

Yours sincerely
Oscar Brittle
Killara

by *The Australian*

Dear Editor,

I have just killed two proverbial birds with one proverbial
stone.

I have just placed a sign on my letterbox saying 'PLEASE
DESTROY'. Not only will this provide the young with an
alternative amusement to stabbing each other: it will ensure
that I no longer receive bad news about frequent increases
in interest rates, bank fees and government charges.

Yours sincerely
Oscar Brittle
Killara

by *The Adelaide Advertiser*

Dear Editor,

There seem to be in your fair city various bees in proverbial bonnets about the construction of a dragway.

Quite apart from the boost to local tourism and retail profits, dragway racing performs an essential social function, similar to kickboxing, hockey **and (at least in the old days) hangings.** Events like these allow people to let off steam, to offload a bit of excess **tostestorone.** I don't know which prison I would be in now if I hadn't taken part in all of these activities at some time.

Anyone who seeks to prevent Canberrans and others from opening the throttle on their automotive super machines will have me to contend with. I look forward to the day when I can bring Ol' Bertha down to the new Canberra Dragstrip and let her rip. There'll be egg (and carbon fumes) on the face of anyone who is there to protest, that's for sure. They'll find out the hard way the veracity of the maxim that appears on Bertha's bumper sticker: Life begins at 140 (mph)!

Yours sincerely
Oscar Brittle
Killara

/ **SOUTHSIDE**
The Chronicle
TUESDAY, DECEMBER 5, 2006

Support for dragway

EDITOR

There seem to be in your fair city various bees in proverbial bonnets about the construction of a dragway. Quite apart from the boost to local tourism and retail profits, dragway racing performs an essential social function, similar to kickboxing and hockey. Events like these allow people to let off steam, to offload a bit of excess testosterone.

I don't know which prison I would be in now if I hadn't taken part in all of these activities at some time.

Anybody who seeks to prevent Canberrans and others from opening the throttle on their automotive super machines will have me to contend with. I look forward to the day when I can bring Ol' Bertha down to the new Canberra Dragstrip and let her rip. There'll be egg (and carbon fumes) on the face of anyone who is there to protest, that's for sure. They'll find out the hard way the veracity of the maxim that appears on Bertha's bumper sticker: Life begins at 140 (mph)!

Oscar Brittle
Killara

Dear Editor,

As one who has fought tooth and nail for integrity in advertising, I am saddened to see today's advertisers throwing around percentages with gay abandon.

When shampoo advertisers claim that their product produces '99.99% less flakiness', or when some sort of bathroom cleansing resin is purported to be '50% tougher on soap scum', perhaps these mathematical cowboys don't expect to be called on it.

Well, Editor, that's exactly what I've been doing this week, only to find that the people at these companies have no idea what I'm talking about. When I requested scientific evidence at one particular place, I was told by a receptionist that she did not know what a percentage was. At another establishment, I was told by a rather listless chap that his 'care factor [was] 0%', whilst another (I won't name names as such) told me he'd like to 'come round and jam a cricket bat 90% of the way up [my] colon'.

I can handle defensiveness (the military taught me that) but what I cannot countenance is the loss of rigour in a once proud and noble profession (advertising).

Yours sincerely
Oscar Brittle
Killara

by *The Newcastle Herald*

Dear Editor,

'Have a nice day!'
    That's what they say to me now when I buy the milk and bread.
    Only God and baby Jesus know why we have to follow the Americans on everything. Wars are one thing (they stimulate the economy), but with many other things we Australians are, to borrow a phrase from the learned Senator Boswell, on a SLIPPERY SLOPE. Thanks to our American friends, pornography in this country is rife, along with 'hop-hop' music, baseball caps, chewing gum, television shows about weight loss, and the incorrect spelling of words like colour, gaol and programme.
    But this 'Have a nice day!' fad is the last proverbial straw. It's as bad as 'How's your day been so far?' when you're waiting for your Golden American Express card to be processed. Do these people really care? Patently not, as demonstrated this afternoon by a pimply face of indifference when I related how I had just stepped in dog excreta, that my sister had narrowly failed in her bid to be elected to the CWA Executive, and that I had been troubled all day by an itchy and painful abscess on my rectum.
    Life is challenging enough without having to explain the ups and downs of my miserable existence to some greasy-haired, text-messaging, church-dodging vagrant who has never picked up a Dickens or Trollope, let alone read it.

Yours sincerely
Oscar Brittle
Killara

by The Australian

Dear Editor,

Lately I've been looking to buy some insect spray, but all I can find is the 'low-irritant' variety. I am wondering if any of your readers could tell me where I can buy the 'high-irritant' version, as I've had no luck whatsoever in my dealings with the manufacturers. It's just that I've been getting a few unwanted guests around my place these days **(namely my infuriating, asthmatic cousin Dallas)** who could do with a bit of irritating.

Yours sincerely
Oscar Brittle
Killara

The Sydney Morning Herald

FRIDAY, AUGUST 4, 2006

COLUMN8

■■■■■■■■

'**Lately** I've been looking to buy some insect spray, but all I can find is the low-irritant variety,' laments Oscar Brittle, of Killara. 'I am wondering if any of your readers could tell me where I can buy the high-irritant version, as I've had no luck whatsoever in my dealings with the manufacturers. It's just that I've been getting a few unwanted guests around my place these days ... who could do with a bit of irritating.'

Dear Editor,

I was recently loaned a book called *The Game*. It proffers advice for picking up women. I have to tell you that I have never read such a load of drivel in my entire life. How any young man hopes to attract the opposite sex using the techniques bandied about by the author is beyond me. He suggests techniques such as 'extradition to a seduction location' and 'pumping buying temperature'. What the hell is that?!

Personally, I've always found success using tried and true methods like the Double Bluff, the Eshenka Twist and the Bohemial Rankle. I've even been known to employ the Varassic Swak on the odd occasion. But more about that in my soon-to-be-released book *Men Have Penises, Women Have Volvos*. It's full of good, practical advice for the would-be philanderer.

I'll be sure to send your magazine a copy once it's published. Consider it a gift - a good review will suffice as payment.

Thanks in advance.

Yours sincerely
Oscar Brittle
Killara

by *FHM* magazine

Dear Editor,

There's no pleasing some people.

If they're not complaining about a lack of rain, they're moaning about a surfeit of the stuff. A handful of flooded buildings, a few dozen dead livestock and one or two drownings, and it seems some would prefer a return to drought conditions!

You didn't hear me grumbling when one of my glasshouses ('Orchids South') sprung a sizeable leak in the most recent thunderstorm, or when the grandchildren stomped through my laundry with muddy wellies, or when my newly detailed Range Rover ended up with unsightly watermarks on the roof and bonnet. To my credit, I soldiered on.

The Greenies can't have it both ways. Storms happen and so do droughts – and it has nothing whatsoever to do with globalisation or warm ocean currents or El Nemo. It's simply a matter of luck. Full stop.

Yours sincerely
Oscar Brittle
Killara

by *The Newcastle Herald*

APRIL 2007

ENTREPRENEUR

Dear Editor, recently I purchased a second-hand surfboard, then sold it for a higher price with no value added whatsoever. In fact, in real terms it had probably depreciated having aged by one week. All this took was six days of salesmanship and a powerful marketing campaign across all local media hinging on a mind-worm of a slogan that won't be forgotten around here for a long time. We achieved 100% saturation. Yours sincerely,

Oscar Brittle

Cool Oscar, but if that's how you get your kicks, Then I think you need to find someway to occupy your time a little better. – Mitch

Dear Editor (Mitch),

Thank you for publicising my successful campaign to sell my surfboard. I should mention that it was only because a friend of my son's saw it _by chance_ on a flight to Phuket that I saw it in print at all. I distinctly told you **in bold** to reply to my email with publication details. Never mind – no harm done.

You said (in print) that 'you [I] need to find some way to occupy your [my] time a little better'. Thanks for the advice, but I think you'll find - if you do your research - that my time is already _of a premium_.

If I'm not on the bowling green, the polo field or at my salsa class, I'm generally travelling. In the current financial year (the only year I recognise), I have been curling in Banff, rescuing Sun Bears in Cambodia (with my wife) and tracking the aurora borealis across Norway, sampling the local mead and bedding down with the locals as I went. I work part-time now, and perhaps you – like the Treasurer – are right to hold me in contempt for that, but when I am working I'm researching the link between halogen lights and obesity, or I'm assisting in the repatriation of returned UN peacekeepers. A bit more important than catching a few waves and butchering the English language, don't you think?

Anyway, no hard feelings, 'Mitch'. Keep working hard on what my son tells me is a hectic mag, bro.

Yours sincerely
Oscar Brittle
Killara

e(lectric)mail

From: *Waves magazine*
To: *Brittle, Oscar*
Subject: *Your letter*

G'day Oscar, how's things? I hope easter treated you and the family well. Sorry for the late reply, but I've been indisposed in recent times and have only just returned to the office. I saw your response to the letter that Mitch published in our April issue of *Waves*. Congratulations on your profit. It would appear you've got a very crafty knack of making a quick buck. Furthermore, I can assure you that Mitch's printed response was completely in jest. The editorial of the magazine is historically comical and Mitch's words were very much aligned with this tone and not reflective of personal opinion exercising malice. A joking response, I can assure.

Furthermore, I'm curious to your reply and whether your words are formed from a joking and/or sarcastic standpoint? 'Keep working hard on what my son tells me is a hectic mag, bro,' and, 'A bit more important than butchering the English language, don't you think?' has somewhat puzzled me. Please pass my thanks onto your son for his loyal readership and if you wish to clarify your above quoted text (or gain further clarification from myself), please contact me.

End of correspondence

Dear Editor,

This is my third day without sleep as part of a self-funded experiment I am calling 'Pushing the Boundaries of Normalcy'.

Right now all I can think of is sleep and how much I want to sleep. I have had dinner and I am inside, so food and shelter are far from my mind: it is only sleep that I crave. I exist only in a realm of base desire. Save for the findings of this experiment I am now completely useless to society, barely able to utter these words for my wife to patiently type. I am primitive. I am naked. Help me.

Yours sincerely
Oscar Brittle
Killara

e(lectric)mails

From: The Editor - The Southern Cross
To: Brittle, Oscar
Subject: Your letter

Dear Mr Brittle,

If you would like a minister to visit you, the Reverend Langley of St John's, Killara, can contact you. I can give you his phone number.

Yours sincerely
The Southern Cross

From: Brittle, Oscar
To: The Editor - The Southern Cross
Subject: Re: Your letter

Thank you, but I won't trouble the Reverend on this occasion. My experiment has concluded and it was a resounding success. Please let me know if your readers would like to hear even more about it.

Yours sincerely
Oscar Brittle

End of correspondence

Times
Milton Ulladulla

SUNDAY, JUNE 4, 2006

Have your say
Posted by Oscar Brittle
Thursday, May 11, 2006

Dear Editor,

What in the name of God is a Lachet? Well that's exactly what I said back in 1997! Please let me explain.

It was seven years ago on a church fellowship field trip that I chanced upon your fishing hamlet of Ulladulla, NSW. I was on the lookout for a nice piece of halibut for my tea. A rather unfortunate-looking woman/fishmonger explained that the only fish available was 'Lachet'.

'What in the name of God is a Lachet?' I enquired politely.

'It's a fish,' hissed the woman. 'You can have 7 Lachet for 7 cents'.

'Sold!' I exclaimed. I trotted home and set about baking a fine fish pie. Dear Editor, it was barely edible.

Upon returning home (Killara), I set about researching the wretched fish. I found no mention of Lachet in any tome. I was outraged – yet quietly intrigued. Had I been sold a furphy by the south coast fishmong? Or had I inadvertently stumbled on a new and as yet unclassified species? I supposed the former and downed tools.

Well, imagine my surprise when, last Friday, I ventured back to Ulladulla and found that Lachet was not a made-up fish! It was back on the menu. I have photographs as proof if you would like to see them (of the fish, not the menu).

I hope this letter has gone some way to answering your questions. If you need any further clarification, please don't hesitate to contact me.

Yours sincerely
Oscar Brittle

(Photograph by O. Brittle, using digital camera)

Dear Editor,

HOT! <u>HOT!</u> HOT!

I am referring, of course, to newsreaderess Sandra Sully.
   Congratulations to the Ten Network for so successfully merging breasts and world events.
   If I wasn't already married to my beloved Pina, I would dearly love to make Sully my wife. I would give her everything. Everything.

Yours sincerely
Oscar Brittle
Killara

by *The Good Weekend*

Dear Editor,

As the result of a negative experience, I would like to warn your readers about the folly of spending large amounts of money for beauty treatments.

Just the other day, I paid more than $305.00 for a 'Chocolate Lover's Delight', hoping that it would allow me to 'escape the mundane' and luxuriate in a 'guilt-free aromatic pampering'. Before I knew it, they had me flat on my back, polishing my body silky smooth with creamy clay mud and fine coffee grounds. This was apparently to assist in 'fluid' retention. Then they cocooned me in a chocolate body wrap and gave me a facial. After showering, I was prostate again, while they massaged me vigorously with a Turkish delight body gel and Tangerine moisture infusion. I don't mind telling you; I was just about ready to take a bite out of myself!

By the time I left I was feeling quite relaxed, if a little 'freaked out' by the whole experience of people smudging me in food. But that's not my point. As soon as I got home, I turned on the television to see that buffoon Harris (Rolf). This caused me to fly into a maniacal rage and, hence, all the benefits I had previously enjoyed were suddenly null and void. If anything, I felt worse than I did prior to my first whiff of choc-mint.

The moral of this story seems to be: $305.00 is a lot to shell out for a short-term gain.

Yours sincerely
Oscar Brittle
Killara

by *The Queanbeyan Age*

Dear Editor,

Parkes has an Elvis Festival. So what?!

My daughter has lived in Dubbo for years and she has long said that the town should embrace the music festival concept. It's so vital for the youngsters, for the businesses and for the profile and reputation of terrific Dubbo.

Her idea is simple yet ingenious: start a *Savage Garden* Festival. This Brisbane supergroup was hugely successful in the mid-to-late 1990s, even travelling to (the United States of) America! Their albums have remained ALMOST CULT-LIKE IN THEIR POPULARITY (according to Nine's Richard Wilkins) and, unlike Presley, this mob is actually Australian. Singer Darren Hayes is a striking (if slightly effeminate-looking) chap and could be effortlessly mimicked by bus-loads of men and women. Heck, after a couple of well-poured whiskies I'd probably have a go myself.

The daughter is a bit shy about engaging in public debate and, as a dab hand, I promised her I'd start the ball rolling with this letter. See what the readers think, hey?! Furthermore, I'd probably be willing to throw some cash at the operation. **(I'm loaded.)**

Yours sincerely
Oscar Brittle
Killara

Daily Liberal

www.dubbo.yourguide.com.au   AND MACQUARIE ADVOCATE

THURSDAY, OCTOBER 26, 2006

Music fest 'truly, madly, deeply' needed in city

Parkes has an Elvis Festival. So what?

My daughter has lived in Dubbo for years and she has long said that the town should embrace the music festival concept. It's so vital for the youngsters, for the businesses and for the profile and reputation of terrific Dubbo.

Her idea is simple yet ingenious: start a Savage Garden Festival. This Brisbane supergroup was hugely successful in the mid-to-late 1990s, even travelling to (the United States of) America!

Their albums have remained 'almost cult-like in their popularity' (according to Nine's Richard Wilkins) and, unlike Presley, this mob is actually Australian.

Singer Darren Hayes is a striking (if slightly effeminate-looking) chap and could be effortlessly mimicked by bus-loads of men and women. Heck, after a couple of well-poured whiskies I'd probably have a go myself.

The daughter is a bit shy about engaging in public debate and, as a dab hand, I promised her I'd start the ball rolling with this letter.

See what the readers think, hey? Furthermore, I'd probably be willing to throw some cash at the operation.

Oscar Brittle
Killara

e(lectric)mails

From: Brittle, Oscar
To: The Editor - The Daily Liberal
Subject: Savage Garden Festival

Hello.

Any response?

Oscar Brittle

From: The Editor – The Daily Liberal
To: Brittle, Oscar
Subject: Re: Savage Garden Festival

Oscar - Not a sausage!! … Care to do a follow-up letter?

Dear Editor,

For the sake of my daughter (and for tax purposes) I remain committed to throwing my formidable financial weight and sheer buying-power behind a music festival for Dubbo and its environs.

This is despite the fact that my original suggestion of a *Savage Garden* Festival received a response from your readers that was lukewarm at best and contemptible at worst. True, the Garden had only nine bona fide classics (compared to Elvis's fifteen) and were always more popular on the coast than they were in the country, but it's not every day someone offers to commemorate an international SUPERGROUP in a regional centre. I would repeat here what the band members themselves said when I told them about this appalling situation, but I don't think it is fit for the consumption of ladies.

Anyway, I thought I'd encourage your readership to write in with its thoughts on the following options for a festival theme. Here they are:

a) E.L.O.
b) Boom Crash Opera
3) Celine Deon
d) Wa Wa Nee
e) Dannii Minogue.

All have been highly successful in their fields, winning more than a dozen major awards between them, and all have been long-standing favourites of the daughter.

Regardless of which artist(s) (yes, we could combine) your readers select, I can almost certainly get Brian Henderson to emcee the event. He's owed me one since '86.

If I hit a wall of apathy again, however, I'm afraid I'll be forced to take my idea to Coonabarrabran. I hear the people there can recognise a good deal when they see it.

Yours sincerely
Oscar Brittle
Killara

Dear Editor,

The fact that Australians annually spend more on toys for their pets than they do on toys for their children was greeted by a mixture of shock and derision by the painted, smiling freaks on one of those morning television shows. I want to know why the aforementioned statistic is so difficult to fathom.

In my experience, children are infernal ingrates who should be hauled from the toy shops and drug parlours and hurled into the lifesavers, scouts or military cadets. Animals, on the other hand, appreciate gifts like they appreciate everything, and their humility and loyalty makes one want to reward them again and again. It's perfectly natural.

What many people probably don't realise is that plants show emotion also, and can benefit from receiving gifts. My camellias get moderately priced jewellery at Christmas and chocolate eggs at Easter (crushed and sprinkled on to their roots), and they seem to shoot up an extra inch with appreciation.

This festive season, I've knitted my pet rock a winter jumpsuit. It's a trial, so I'll be sure to let you know how he reacts. (It's okay - he can't read so it will still be a surprise.)

Yours sincerely
Oscar Brittle
Killara

by *The Launceston Examiner*

Dear Editor,

A question: How do the police ever expect to catch any
criminals when they are all so horrendously FAT? I saw one
the other day that was so porky he could barely breathe!
Even at my age, I would back myself to outpace Fatty over
sixty yards.

Yours sincerely
Oscar Brittle
Killara

by *The North Shore Times*

The Chronicle
SOUTHSIDE

TUESDAY, SEPTEMBER 5, 2006

Backyard clean-up

EDITOR

CHIEF Minister Stanhope is keen to have Sydney residents relocate to Canberra. Good idea. But perhaps he needs to clean up his own backyard before he lobs onto the doorsteps of Campbelltowners.

I visit my daughter regularly in your city and the other day I and my clipboard conducted a detailed survey of her (southern) suburb to see just how desirable it would be to newcomers. Without naming the suburb, I am more than happy to report the following facts: 117 cracked footpath slabs, six fallen gum trees, two burnt out cars, two dead animals, 49 defaced fences, four damaged street lights, nine unruly teenagers letting off firecrackers, 11 piles of dog faeces, six roaming dogs, 10 roaming cats, one roaming ferret, 14 upturned wheelie bins, five emptied ashtrays, 16 skidmarks, three destroyed letter-boxes, three loud stereos, four swooping birds and one abusive resident (female).

Oscar Brittle
Killara

Dear Editor,

It is rare these days that I am shocked. Yesterday I was shocked.

I was searching the electric Internet for some information concerning the ancient Japanese art of bonsai when I stumbled upon a website called 'www.bonsaiyourpet. com'.

Who, I ask, bonsais their pet?!

I cannot tell you much about this abomination as I promptly commenced a bout of dry retching and needed to leave the site post-haste. From what I gathered, one uses a variety of cruel tools to shave, bend and crimp one's dog, cat or horse until they are a miniature version of their previous self! One of the 'after' pictures showed a rabbit that could fit inside a soft drink can!!

The experience has made me deeply cynical about the hearts of men. If ever I meet the cads who dreamt up this ghastly muck I think I'd like to bonsai their testicles for them. That seems to be the only language these people understand.

Yours sincerely
Oscar Brittle
Killara

by *The New Yorker*

Dear Editor,

I just wanted to warn your readers (and you) about some shysters out there.

The other day I opened some mail to find the word 'Congratulations!'. I was filled with hope. I read further. 'You have won!' it said. I kept reading, my lips moistening. 'One of these prizes is definitely yours!'. I was hooked.

The prizes, one of which was <u>definitely</u> mine, consisted of $10,000 cash, a Sony Play Station, an Apple Ipod, a digital camera, a CD player, $500 cash or a magic sketcher key ring. All I had to do was buy one of their products.

Perhaps it was naïve of me, but I calculated that I had a one in seven chance of winning any of these prizes. As it turned out, I won the magic sketcher key ring. I must admit - this disappointed me.

Anyway, that night at the club I spoke to four people who had entered exactly like me. All of them had also won the magic sketcher key ring. In my opinion, this is no coincidence. I am convinced that they are giving these things to everyone. They probably have a thousand of them, all made for a pittance by some miserable wretch somewhere in the Far East. I wonder if anybody is winning the $10,000, or the Apple Ipod for that matter. I suspect not. And my suspicions, I hasten to add, are usually correct.

Yours sincerely
Oscar Brittle
Killara

by *The Penrith Star*

Dear Editor,

I know it shouldn't bother someone like me, but it does.

The purchasing classes have become rather good these days at whingeing and rather less good at old-fashioned enterprise. An interest rate hike or increase in fuel prices is no cause for bowed heads, snivelling or attacking the pollies. Things like this should be seen as <u>challenges</u>, and it's not only me who thinks this – my wife agrees!

My father was in the stink they called the Great Depression, and he used to sell dead rabbits to those who couldn't afford grouse or venison. Similarly, my mother managed to earn a few shillings by mucking in with some of the army boys in the year Hitler sent the Frogs scurrying across the pond.

If cash flow is a problem, the young need to think laterally and imaginatively. I encouraged my son to get into the fight game to earn a few extra bob. He's 'one and eleven' at present, but he's only been knocked out twice and even the losers get a generously sized counter meal after the doctor has seen them. And my youngest niece (a simple girl) is, with my assistance, currently negotiating a price with an Argentinean family for one of her kidneys. As I've said for weeks now, when one kidney is enough to do the job, the second must be seen as a gift from God – and money in the bank!

There is plenty of cash in the world – you've just got to know where to look for it. Nothing ever came to those who sit around waiting for their pools numbers to come up, or to those who insist on harking back to the days of plenty.

Yours sincerely
Oscar Brittle
Killara

by *The Illawarra Mercury*

North Shore Times

FRIDAY, MARCH 17, 2006

A lot of blinking trouble

ONE thing I notice when I'm driving the Volvo around my neighbourhood (apart from the proliferation of Labradors) is the number of imported prestige vehicles with faulty indicators.

I have lost count of the number of BMW and Mercedes-Benz cars that seem to have this problem.

Jaguars too! I've had not a day's grief with my Volvo's indicators in the 24 years I've owned her.

And I must have turned four score or more corners during that time. Considering the price tag on these imported automobiles, I would have thought indicator trouble unacceptable. But I hear no complaint from their owners.

I wonder if other readers have noticed this phenomenon.

Oscar Brittle
Killara

Dear Editor,

There seems to be an awful lot of sex on the television at the moment.

A few months ago I was watching SBS at 2.30 in the morning, when a couple began fornicating right there on the screen. They were wearing very little, if any, clothing. The woman's breasts were clearly visible but, to be fair, I could not see genitalias. The whole experience shocked me, but I was prepared to let it slide on the grounds that few people would see it if it was on so late. I am rarely up so late myself!

It is a different story with *Big Brother Adults Only*, which appears at 9.30pm, just after prime time. Genitals can quite easily be seen on this program, particularly male ones. And it is not unknown for women (lesbians) to kiss each other on the lips.

Call me prudish, but I think society is damned if this sort of outlandish behaviour is not confined to the bedroom or living room. It certainly should not be televised nationally, as is the current state of affairs.

If you or your readers do not respond to this letter, I will assume you agree with me.

Yours sincerely
Oscar Brittle
Killara

e(lectric)mails

From: The Editor - The Southern Cross
To: Brittle, Oscar
Subject: Your letter

Dear Mr Brittle,

I am sorry to say that your letter could not be published in *Southern Cross*, in part due to space limitations.

Our general guidelines are that letters should respond to an issue raised in a recent edition of the newspaper. It will ensure that your letter makes the short list if it engages with these criteria, as we receive a large volume of letters. While your letter raised an important issue in our society, it did not engage directly with an article in *Southern Cross*. I would encourage you to continue writing.

I hope you find this useful and thank you for your support of *Southern Cross*.

Best regards
The Southern Cross

From: Brittle, Oscar
To: The Editor – The Southern Cross
Subject: Re: Your Letter

I humbly take this 'on the chin' and I promise to write again ... often!

Yours sincerely
Oscar Brittle
Killara

End of correspondence

Dear Editor,

'Viagra is a wonderful drug!' they say.

Well, try telling that to my todger, which has been as hard as a proverbial rock for (at the time of writing) thirty-four hours. The persistent throb is crippling, despite my wife's best efforts.

It's time the quacks got it right, don't you think?

Yours sincerely
Oscar Brittle
Killara

by *Ralph* magazine

Dear Editor,

Another day, another news item about that grinning American midget, Tom Cruise, and this time it's about his bizarre purchase of a Mexican walking fish. Frankly, I'd be more interested in news about the fish than its master.

Perhaps one learns most about Cruise through an analysis of the company he keeps: the overpaid, skirt-wearing soccer player with the silly voice and anorexic wife; the white singer who used to be black, who shares his bed with underprivileged minors and 'Bubbles' the orangutan; the aging, wig-wearing pop singer who too freely offers his sizeable middle digit to security staff at Asian airports; as well as a small but loyal flock of aliens whom he has met through his Scientography.

Normal people like me don't bother with the clown.

Yours sincerely
Oscar Brittle
Killara

by *The Los Angeles Daily News*

Dear Editor,

I turned on the television on Saturday morning **and nearly fell off my perch … literally.**

It's been years since I've seen a 'video clip'. In fact, I think the last one I saw was introduced by that Molly person with the strange hat and it was on the ABC. I remember thinking that that particular clip was **(like the show's host)** filth, but, when I think about it, the most suggestive aspect of the clip was a pair of impossibly tight trousers torturing a small-medium package.

Lo and behold, video clips have come a long way in 25 years. On Saturday, for three horrible hours, I watched in disgust and denial as young women gallivanted about the place in tiny swimsuits, brassieres, underpants and other garments that a man should only see in the boudoir. Males too, it seems, have gotten in on the act, showing off the tops of their bottoms with apparent impunity.

Recent research shows that young people are having sex (especially oral) younger and younger. Is it any wonder? There must be a lot of boys who can't wait for Saturday morning to roll around. The little beggars must be bursting out of their strides and that's the very last thing society needs.

Yours sincerely
Oscar Brittle
Killara

TUESDAY, OCTOBER 3, 2006

Red-hot morning

I turned on the television on Saturday morning and saw a video clip for the first time in years. I think the last one I saw was introduced by that Molly person with the strange hat and it was on the ABC.

I remember thinking that that particular clip was filth, but, when I think about it, the most suggestive aspect of the clip was a pair of impossibly tight trousers torturing a small-medium package. Lo and behold, video clips have come a long way in 25 years.

On Saturday, for three horrible hours, I watched in disgust and denial as young women gallivanted about the place in tiny swimsuits, brassieres, underpants and other garments that a man should only see in the boudoir.

Males too, it seems, have gotten in on the act, showing off the tops of their bottoms with apparent impunity.

Recent research shows that young people are having sex (especially oral) younger and younger. Is it any wonder?

There must be a lot of boys who can't wait for Saturday morning to roll around. The little beggars must be bursting out of their strides – and that's the very last thing society needs.

Oscar Brittle
Killara

Also published by *The Sunday Herald Sun* under the title 'Video Sex'

WEDNESDAY, OCTOBER 4, 2006

What's new

In response to Oscar Brittle ('Red-hot morning,' *Letters*, October 3), I am sure teenagers have been having sex ever since they have had hormones.

What has changed in the last 60 years is that people are more open about their sexuality and data collection is a lot more widespread.

Another point is to look at cultures that marry out their daughters as soon as they become 'women'. A lot of them are mere teenagers.

These cultures are thousands of years old, yet I am sure these girls were having sex on their wedding night.

Troy Butler
Richmond

Dear Editor,

Okay, I have something on my mind that I need to get off my chest. And that something is 'Intelligent Design'. Or, as I like to call it, 'ID'.

When it comes to cognitive fortitude (IQ) I am well above the lowest common denominator. Or so I'm led to believe.

Anyway, what's got me thinking is this: How can Homo Sapiens (I use this term advisedly) as a genus/species believe in something like 'ID' when the majority of them can't even get into a lift properly?

I've lost count (literally) of the times that I've been in a lift, it's gotten to my floor, I've prepared myself mentally to exit the lift once the doors open, and have been prevented by a group of idiom blocking my exit and trying to get into the lift before I've gotten out! Surely sanity dictates that they should step aside and let me out first. My salient message to humanity is this: 'Hurry up and evolve'! Opposable thumbs alone aren't good enough any more if you don't want to miss the so-called 'boat'.

You'll be excited to learn that I have expanded my philosophy to include escalators, trains and footpaths and I'm putting the final touches to my manifestos before sending them to MENSA with instructions to read said documentum.

Thanks again for your support of my important work. I'll keep you posted as things develop!

Yours sincerely
Oscar Brittle
Killara

REJECTED

by *The Christian Science Monitor*

The Diary

AMANDA MEADE

THURSDAY, OCTOBER 26, 2006

An Oscar for best actor

DIARY calls on prolific letter writer **'Oscar Brittle** of Killara' to identify himself. After a series of curious letters were published in *The Daily Telegraph*, we tried to verify that Brittle was a real person. Here is Brittle on public transport: 'The morning trip was pleasant enough, as I sat next to a handsome, lightly perfumed young woman, read the paper and even attempted a Sudoku puzzle.' And on music video on television: 'Recent research shows that young people are having sex (especially oral) younger and younger. Is it any wonder? There must be a lot of boys who can't wait for Saturday morning to roll around. The little beggars must be bursting out of their strides – and that's the very last thing society needs.' The opinionated Brittle is not listed in the White Pages and he does not exist on the electoral roll. But he has popped up in *Column 8* in *The Sydney Morning Herald* and on the letter pages of *The Australian*. So beware, letters editors everywhere, there may be another phantom on the loose.

Dear Editor,

Apologies for not writing sooner. I have been somewhat out of the loop of late, getting back to basics at my little bungalow in the Grampians. My chum Colin tells me, via electric mail, that last week Ms Amanda Meade wrote a short piece about me in her column. He says I should be flattered, but I'm not so sure.

I have been called a fool, a drifter and a scallywag in my time, but never a phantom!

Ms Meade is correct in stating that I am not on the electoral roll. My years farming eels in Marrakech taught me the folly of voting. You will only ever replace a tyrant with a tyrant. I wish them all to slippery hell.

As far as the 'White Pages' is concerned, I believe one qualifies by 'listing' a telephone number. Since '97, speaking on the phone has just been too painful for me. (I'd rather not discuss what happened in that year of living dangerously.)

Still, you can't keep a good man down. They tried that with Pitt the Younger, with Disraeli, and with Thatcher. This nation needs *men of the pen* like Brittle and Jones, my dear Editor, and you can look forward to more 'curious' correspondence. Of course, if it is not to the liking of your newspaper's power brokers, you can always depress the 'delete' button on the touch key board in the cyber world you rule. I won't take offence.

Please pass on my thanks to Mrs Meade for her interest in my letters. Colin assures me that she is the most competent and admired of journalists. Personally, I'm not familiar with her work, though I once *drank mead* with a woman of generous bosom in rural Sweden. But that's another story, for another time.

Yours sincerely
Oscar Brittle
Killara

No response

Dear Editor,

Seven houses. Three estates. Prestige cars. Lear jets. (The jets are always rented. If it flies, floats or fornicates, always rent it — it's cheaper in the long run.) Acres of land. Contemporary art on the walls, and stables full of thoroughbreds. Bronze statues littering the garden. Butlers, chefs, chauffeurs, financial advisers and other personal staff coming out of my posterior. Oh, and thousands of bottles of Champagne in the cellars. You can never have enough Champagne.

Making money was, and still is, fun. It consumes my waking hours. My lifestyle is one of class A drugs, high-class escorts, drink and flamboyant debauchery.

Whoever said money doesn't buy happiness is a fool. I'm as happy as an expensive pig in very expensive shit.

Yours sincerely
Oscar Brittle
Killara

by *The Wall Street Journal*

Dear Editor,

Stop the nation – I want to get off!

    If one reads, listens to or views mainstream media these days (and, let's face it, who can possibly avoid it) one quickly arrives at the conclusion that Australia has finally been overrun with penny-pinching politicians, corporate devils, tax auditors, do-nothing celebrities, video disc jockeys, overpaid sportsmen, incompetent referees and parking inspectors. These are not people with whom I choose to associate and, as a consequence, I'm off.

    I intend to found a brand new sovereign country on a small, barren patch of unoccupied territory adjacent to Burkina Faso (in Africa and, coincidentally, not far from you). In this new nation, tentatively named 'Oscar Brittle', I will rule firmly but benevolently; the practical medium of money will be forgone in favour of the ideal of neighbourly trust, and the weak will not be welcome. Life will be simple but so very beautiful in Oscar Brittle (the country).

    I encourage your readers to keep their eyes and ears peeled for a powerful advertising campaign starting next month. Recruitment offices will be set up in each state (except Queensland).

Yours sincerely
Oscar Brittle
Killara

by *The West Australian*

Dear Editor,

If you ask me, it's about time the mob at the Oxford English Dictionary got its act together.

The precedent of including verbs derived from proper nouns, such as **google** (to search for something on the internet), **hoover** (to vacuum something) or even **delia** (to cook something, apparently) is well established. Agreed. So, why are these Oxford chaps baulking at my proposal to broaden the definition of the word **brittle**?

Everybody knows that **brittle** is already in the dictionary, as an adjective ('apt to break, fragile') and as a noun ('sweet made from nuts and melted sugar'). But I would like it in there as a *verb*! The amendment I've proposed is:

brittle 3. *v.* to perform a task flawlessly, to perfection.

People who know me (in the northern suburbs of Sydney, Australia) have been using the term **brittle** in this way for years. A perfect lawn bowl might be greeted with the words: 'He's **brittled** it!' A request for a faultless submission in the office is often followed by the reminder: 'Make sure you **brittle** it.' When a function runs smoothly it is often said to have been '**brittled**'. I contend that such lingo is common, perhaps not as common as **google**, but certainly more so than **delia**.

I'm not saying *I'm* perfect, but everybody up this way knows that *the things I do* often are. It's a talent passed on from my grandfather Axel Brittle, who rarely put a foot wrong – until his inglorious demise in the port town of Suva back in '36.

So, get it together Oxford, or I'll be forced to talk to Collins, or Macquarie, or Websters – or even Funk & Wagnall.

Yours sincerely
Oscar Brittle
Killara

by *The London Times*

Dear Editor,

Nagasaki. Petrov. Vietnam. Rwanda. Iraq.

Monroe. Mount batten. Castro.

Pentagon. Pyramid.

Harrier Jump Jet.

It's the lies I don't like.

Politicians' lies. A tautology? Maybe.

Once, in '91, I sat across from one at a cozy little
luncheon, paid for by me. He implied that he'd 'fix' a little
property deal if I kept quiet. And did he? No. Why? In
prison. Why? Lies. And so it goes.

Big fish need frying. It's time to fry.

Yours sincerely
Oscar Brittle
Killara

by *The Otago Daily*, NZ

The Mosman Daily

THURSDAY, OCTOBER 19, 2006

Teach students classic texts

I have it on good authority that some teachers are now exposing senior students to communist propaganda from Latin America, the left-wing ravings of that lunatic filmmaker Michael Moore, Gonzo writing by substance-abusing troublemakers such as Hunter S. Thomson, and even blogs by young people telling the world (with abysmal punctuation) how great they are.

I've said it before in these pages and I'll say it again – this is not literature!

Literature is about the canon: the work of writers who have stood the test of time and inspired generations with their charm, insight and respect for convention.

Occasionally a new writer will be added to this select group, perhaps a Le Carre or an Atwood.

But in the main, the canon remains untainted.

It is only when students read the likes of Chaucer, Donne, Shakespeare, Dickens, Hardy, Austen, Brittle, Eliot, Paterson and Lawson that they acquire the wisdom to navigate their way through a complex world.

And it's becoming more and more complex.

Oscar Brittle
Killara

The Mosman Daily

THURSDAY, NOVEMBER 9, 2006

I commend Oscar Brittle's critique of left-wing and obese Michael Moore and gonzo author Hunter Thompson, who in a cocainised state would reverse at speed out of his driveway in his red roadster and race past the police precinct to their dismay (*Daily*, October 19). I agree with Oscar Brittle's advocacy of reading the classic authors. Oscar Brittle did not mention the need for an anti-virus to expunge the virus known as critical literacy. Leftist teachers ask pupils to examine literature from the point of view of Marxism, feminism and power relations. Critical literacy is reminiscent of 'newspeak' in Orwell's *1984*. I wonder what is the incidence of critical literacy in schools on the North Shore?

Alan Grant
McMahons Point

Dear Editor,

A lot of society's heavyweights have had their say in the debate on manners and common decency, yet I have not. It is now that I choose to break my silence.

Many a well-poured evening whiskey has been interrupted of late by outsourced foreigners calling me with fantastical fables of unbeatable (tele)phone deals. I have, to this point, tolerated the incursion on the grounds that the poor wretches are just trying to eke out a living in nations beset by problems of La Nino, pollution, overpopulation, scarcity of resources and appalling cinema.

Last Wednesday, I'm afraid, my patience evaporated, the direct result of one of these coves addressing me not as 'Mr. Brittle' (as one should expect) but as 'Oscar'. <u>Not even my housekeeper dares breathe that name to me.</u> Such familiarity will only be accepted from my mother, my lawyer, my broker and my wife Pina (though strictly in the home). The right to be called 'Mr. Brittle' is, for me, the very last bastion of formality and a matter on which I am not prepared to compromise. The caller, claiming to be called 'Dilip', found this out the hard way when I forcefully pressed the OFF button in his impertinent ear.

I hereby issue a first and last warning to all service providers, retailers and salesmen – here and abroad. Addressing me by my Christian name will illicit the same response as if one was to call me 'mate', 'buddy', 'champ', 'love' or 'darl'. This response will be swift, decisive and unapologetically vicious.

Yours sincerely
Mr. Oscar Brittle
Killara

by *The Northern Daily Leader*

Dear Editor,

What do reality television shows and theme parks have in common? You're an intelligent man so you'll excuse my rhetoric. As we both know, they are responsible for the lowering of morals in this country. I have no solution for the first (stupid is as stupid does) but for the latter I have a clever panacea.

My idea is to open my own chain of theme parks. I will call these parks 'The Real World'. The populace seems more than happy to pay exorbitant admission prices to enter theme parks such as Disneyland, Dreamworld and Funland (Ulladulla), so it is my plan to charge a comparable fee at the exits of these establishments before allowing people entry back into 'The Real World'. Forget roller-coasters and big dippers - patrons of 'The Real World' will enjoy attractions including, but not limited to: death, taxes, commercial television, speed cameras, homophobia, xenophobia, and misogyny (old Walt would have been proud!). In short, REALITY! It's the only way to make the purchasing classes appreciate how good they have it and to think twice before hastily forking out to enter these centres of manufactured 'fun'.

There is a sign outside Disneyland which arrogantly proclaims it is 'The Happiest Place on Earth'. I won't stand for such erroneous signage outside 'The Real World'™. On the contrary, I plan to manage expectations with the more appropriate 'The Real World - Cruel but Necessary' in blazing neon.

I start work on the finer details of my enterprise tomorrow. Look out for the press release and complimentary 'The Real World' tickets for you and your family (valued at over €49.95). I look forward to seeing you in 'The Real World' some time soon!

Yours sincerely
Oscar Brittle
Killara

by *The Age*

MONDAY, FEBRUARY 12, 2007

It's all in the editing

I have noticed that some newspaper editors have been taking the edit part of their job title rather too zealously. Some of my recent efforts have been crudely and mercilessly culled, to the point where the subtleties have been lost. In one case (not in this paper) a reference to the word "hanging" was totally removed, and all this in a democracy! The message is that the editor knows better than me what I want to say, a message that many would brand as gross impertinence. However, I am harder to offend than most.

Below is a list of words I was planning to use in a letter. Do with it what you will. It's easier this way: Oil, the, in, crisis, silicone, Bush, alleviate, minerals, a, minutes, yearling, wealth, whiskey, stock, crisis, embargo, outside, scandal, shipping, very, Farouk, relations, edict, mind-worm, an, interest, Mountbatten, spectacular, corrupt.

If time gets away from you I suggest you cut and paste it across to the puzzles page. The regulars might appreciate a change. Alternatively, create a competition, and the correspondent who most faithfully recreates the letter you feel I would be most likely to write could edit your paper for, say, a week.

Oscar Brittle
Killara, NSW

As published by *The Australian*

TUESDAY, FEBRUARY 13, 2007

Oscar Brittle, I hope for your sake that your complaint (12/2) about your letters being edited was heavily edited by the letters editor, for I had no idea what you were trying to say. If you understand what I mean.

Dick Garner
Maryborough, Qld

WEDNESDAY, FEBRUARY 14, 2007

Unlike Oscar Brittle (*Letters*, 12/2) the letters submitted by this humble pencil to *The Australian* have not suffered the editing of even a punctuation mark – let alone a single word. In fact, not a single word of any letter submitted has ever been published.

Ian Ward
Yeppoon, Qld

Dear Editor,

When I was a young man, the anus was for expelling things, not inserting them.

Apparently, shafting the drug 'ICE' is the latest vile abomination in this regard. Perhaps doctors inspired this with their bizarre suppository obsession – who knows?

...

My cousin Dallas, whose stories admittedly require vigilant checking, says that he recently heard an Emergency Department nurse say that a male patient had been admitted courtesy of a rectum packed with a soup ladle, a small inflatable beach ball and a tradesman's tool kit including a Phillips head screwdriver and a slide rule.

Furthermore, a Paris man has reportedly become so distrusting of banks that he keeps wads of bank notes in his back passage.

To think that some people still deny the world is coming to an end.

Yours sincerely
Oscar Brittle
Killara

by *Rolling Stone* magazine

WIRED

JANUARY 2009

IRATE LETTER OF THE MONTH

Note that came to us for no particular reason whatsoever but that we like anyway and reprint here verbatim:

A letter for publication. Please let me know promptly if there is some sort of problem publishing this in your next issue. I'm old, unwell, and won't be around forever.

Dear Editor,

Today I received an electric mail from 'Erection problems' telling me that I had the apparently unique chance to make my 'squib' a 'real space rocket' and raise me up to 'the seventh sky of the sexual satisfaction'.

WHAT THE HELL?!

Of all the impertinent things to offer a man.

We can put an alleged man on an alleged moon, but we can't seem to protect ordinary, law-abiding chaps from great big stinking servings of crass opportunism and depraved filth whilst they try to eat their mid-morning muffin.

Who is responsible for this and can they be punished immediately? Please advise.

Yours sincerely
Oscar Brittle
Killara
AUSTRALIA

Copyright © 2009. All rights reserved.
Originally published in *Wired*. Reprinted by permission.

Dear Editor,

I was yabbying at Wodonga last week and, to cut a long story short, my cousin Gladys and her husband Leon talked me into visiting a clairvoyant whom they see from time to time, named Ms Destanee Wilson. At first I was highly skeptical of such mumbo-jumbo and I needed a lot of convincing, but I am now very glad indeed that I went along.

Through a combination of tarot, numerology and crystal-ball analysis, Ms Wilson reported many interesting things about me - one of the most interesting being that I am The Messiah, come to Earth for the second time to save all of the Christians.

Not convinced? Believe me - neither was I. That was until Ms Wilson started producing an array of facts to verify her story. She had many visions in the ball that day, including me carrying a cross on the road to Galilee, me dining with my disciples at the so-called Last Supper and me escaping from that cave with the rock door three days after crucifixion.

She also illuminated things about me which are uncannily Christ-like. For example, I once sported a beard, I once owned a bakery and I have, over the years, hosted countless seafood soirees at my place. Also, my birthday is the 25th of December. That fact alone probably should have rung a bell.

So, where to from here? I guess I'll know more after my follow-up appointment in February, but I imagine I will embark on a speaking tour and meet some world leaders including the Pope and the Archbishop of Canterbury. It looks like we might find out who is right once and for all!

Yours sincerely
Jesus Brittle
Killara

by *The Sydney Morning Herald*

Brittle HQ

Glenn Fowler

Despite the hype, Glenn is really nothing special. He studied history and English at university before becoming a teacher and then a union official. His first book, humbly titled *Glenn Goes Global: Tales of a Footloose Colonial* (2004), may be unknown to *you* but it was massive in the Baltic States. Glenn lives in Canberra with his young family and a 2003 Ford Falcon (station wagon) known affectionately as 'The Lemon'. For a mental picture of Glenn, close your eyes and try to imagine a walking, talking set of powerful biceps. He is the humility behind Oscar Brittle.

Christopher Smyth

Chris is a television and new media producer. He has produced children's, youth, news and comedy programs for the ABC including the now iconic *Chaser News Alert* series. He is a graduate of the Australian Film Television and Radio School, where he studied histrionics. He is a director of Big Red Tractor Productions, a small television production company (with a nice website). In his spare time, Chris pretends to be a surfer and he enjoys jogging and pesto. Oscar Brittle is Chris's life coach and is helping him 'live the dream'.

Gareth Malone

Growing up beneath Canberra's inspiring sunsets in a household filled with books, records and musical instruments, Gareth gained a sensitivity to the interconnectedness of all life forms, an appreciation for 'The Golden Age of Jazz' and an ability to envisage future lands beyond dreams. In the mornings you'll find him swimming lazily with the rising sun and in the evenings singing lead vocals for a popular group whose music he describes as: 'romantic ... the lyrics clearly feature animals speaking, though it's not loud ... many notes roam soft, wild and heady with innocent goodness.' Oscar Brittle plays the band's latest recording in his Mirror Room during long nights of reflection fuelled with the finest of imbibements. Gareth's contributions appear on pages 27, 44, 49, 65, 80–81, 95, 110–111, 122 and 126.

Acknowledgments

Thanks, in an alphabetically correct fashion, to Phillip Adams, Grahame Bond, John Doyle and Chris Taylor for seeing something in this project.

Thanks to superbly talented illustrator Andrew Joyner for putting a bald head and rotund physique to a silly name (and apologies to anyone who has that silly name).

Thanks to Phillipa McGuinness and the team at UNSW Press for believing as we do (and as all publishers should) that Australian readers want to read something a little bit different.

Thanks to Jane Caro, Sarah Herbert, Deborah Tobias, Peter Cochrane, Clare Hallifax and Kath Philp for advice along the way.

Thanks to all our friends who kept an eye on the papers for Oscar's letters and jubilantly shared their findings with us.

Thanks to those who replied to Oscar's letters and put the icing on the cake.

Thanks to the many newspapers and magazines that permitted us to re-publish material – *AdNews, Adore Animals* (previously *Adore a New Breed*), *Australian Traveller* magazine, *Canberra Times, Daily Liberal, Herald Sun/Sunday Herald Sun, Irrigator, Milton Ulladulla Times, Mosman Daily, National Liquor News, New England Journal of Medicine, Newcastle Herald, North Shore Times, Parramatta Sun, Sydney Morning Herald, Southern Cross, Southside Chronicle, Waves* magazine and

Wired magazine.

Gareth particularly thanks all the letters page editors and newspaper and magazine readers who have attempted to decipher these veiled, ludicrous musings and been forced to ask themselves in near desperation: Could there possibly be such a man as Brittle?

Chris thanks his long-suffering family and friends for enduring the absurdity, the residents of Killara for inspiration and his co-authors for making him laugh.

Glenn thanks his dear friend Jacquie for her wise counsel and unwavering support; Dashiell and Billie for accepting Dadda's indulgences; and Marina, as always.

INDEX